As The World Dies

Untold Tales

Volume One

Rhiannon Frater

As the World Dies: Untold Tales V.1
By Rhiannon Frater

Original Copyright 2008 - 2011 by Rhiannon Frater
All Rights Reserved.

Edited by Felicia A. Sullivan
Interior formatting by Kody Boye
Cover Artwork and Layout by Philip Rogers

ISBN-13:
978-1441440464
ISBN-10:
1441440461

http://rhiannonfrater.com/
http://astheworlddies.com/

Author's Note:

The original *AS THE WORLD DIES* TRILOGY was written over a two year span in a series of mini-chapters that were posted on a somewhat regular schedule. I accidentally began what would be my zombie epic when I quickly wrote down a zombie short story and posted it online. The response to the story was immediately positive and people wanted to know when I would post the rest of it.

I hadn't even considered that there was more to the story, but as the encouraging words continued to hit my email box, I realized there was more story to tell. I traveled far and wide over the great state of Texas for my job as a governmental consultant and spent many hours on the road. My experiences in small towns in Texas inspired me to write my zombie epic about a small town in the middle of Nowhere, Texas where a group of survivors band together to fight the undead and somehow pioneer a new life for themselves.

After successfully self-publishing the *AS THE WORLD DIES* TRILOGY and winning several awards, the series was optioned for a possible film or TV series and was picked up by Tor for reissue. The revised version of *THE FIRST DAYS* was published on July 5, 2011. *FIGHTING TO SURVIVE* is scheduled to be published in November 2011 with *SIEGE* following in the Spring of 2012.

AS THE WORLD DIES UNTOLD TALES VOL 1 is a collection of previously unpublished short stories set in the same world as *THE FIRST DAYS*.

To purchase THE FIRST DAYS: AS THE WORLD DIES, visit:
http://us.macmillan.com/thefirstdays

Or purchase from your favorite online retailer or local bookstore.

Also by Rhiannon Frater

As the World Dies Series
The First Days
Fighting to Survive (November 2011 from Tor)
Siege (Spring 2012 from Tor)

Pretty When She... Series
Pretty When She Dies: A Vampire Novel

Vampire Bride Series
The Tale of the Vampire Bride
The Vengeance of the Vampire Bride

The Living Dead Boy and the Zombie Hunters

Dedicated to the fans of the original online serial and self-published novels. My success is because of your devotion and encouragement. I cannot thank you enough.

Table of Contents

Lydia's Story

Katie Kiel's wife, Lydia, is probably one of the most iconic and beloved characters in the *AS THE WORLD DIES* trilogy, yet she is already dead when the story begins.

Appearing in Katie's memory and as a ghostly manifestation, Lydia's appearance in *THE FIRST DAYS* has a huge impact not only on Katie, but many of the readers as well. After the original self-published books were released, a lot of fans told me how much they enjoyed how Lydia and Katie's love endures beyond death, but many also inquired as to how she died.

At first I thought this was morbid fascination, but then I realized that because Katie never knows how her wife dies, her sad fate is a mystery. Since I wrote the original serial online, I always knew exactly how Lydia died. In fact, I almost rewrote the beginning of the book to include her death. I scrapped this idea when I realized that the sheer power of the opening scene *Tiny Fingers* is what immediately hooks the reader into the *THE FIRST DAYS*.

I originally wrote this short story as a gift to my loyal fans and posted it on my forum. It was very well-received. A lot of the fandom appreciated seeing Katie and Lydia together as a couple before they are torn apart by the zombie rising.

This is the perfect prologue to *THE FIRST DAYS*; therefore, it begins our *Untold Tales*.

The Broken Heart

The last day of Lydia's life started like any other. She woke up next to the woman she loved, rolled over, and snuggled into Katie's warmth. With gentle fingers, she swept Katie's curls back from her sleeping face and placed a soft kiss against her forehead. As usual, Katie remained deeply asleep, not even stirring.

With a smile, Lydia slid out of bed, her long silk nightgown spilling to her feet. She walked to the sliding doors that opened onto the patio overlooking their small section of the lake. The sky was barely graying over the hills and a soft mist flowed over the dark waters. It was a serene view and Lydia inhaled deeply, taking in the quiet beauty of the moment and relishing the awakening of the morning.

Donning her robe, she left the lights off as she strolled to the kitchen enjoying the early morning darkness filling the rooms. It was always lovely to see the house slowly fill with morning light.

As she brewed a cup of mint tea, she left the small TV tucked onto a corner of the counter turned off. She liked keeping the world at bay until the sun was up and the day officially started. Early mornings were for tranquility and meditation.

Once the tea was brewed, she stepped out into the crisp morning air, her cup in one hand. A soft breeze ruffled her short hair as she slid into her meditation chair, setting the cup down on the low table beside her. The fragrance of mint filled the air, aromatic and calming. It was here every morning that she took the time to center herself and prepare for the day ahead. It was her daily ritual and one that brought her tranquility. She straightened her back and slightly closed her eyes. Settling in, she concentrated on her breath, inhaling... exhaling...

A sharp, shrill scream broke through her serenity and her head came up sharply. It had come from across the lake, the echoes of the terrible sound fading away. It was most likely a water bird. Calming her breathing, she tried to focus herself again. Lowering her lashes, she took in a deep breath.

The scream came again, sounding more agonized, and frantic. Lydia rose to her feet, peering across the rippling waters at the still dark houses across the lake. It was most likely a water bird or a cat in distress, but the sound made her skin crawl. She waited, her head tilted, hoping to identify the sound. Feeling strangely unsettled, she took another step toward the lake, the flagstones under her feet still cold from the night chill.

Perhaps it was her imagination, but odd sounds mingled with the gentle lapping of the water against the retaining wall. She continued to strain, trying to hear, all sense of calm leaving her.

Another sudden screech behind her made her jump. Her heart thudding in her chest, she realized it was Katie's alarm wailing. There was a grunt from inside the house, then the alarm clock was silenced. Lights flickered on.

Forcing herself to take three deep breaths, Lydia picked up her cooling cup of tea and ventured inside. Katie was already in their enormous bathroom, washing her face. The tank top and soft silk shorts she wore clung to her athletic frame and her hair was golden in the glow of the lights.

Placing her cup on the marble countertop, Lydia slid her arm around Katie's waist and kissed her shoulder. "Good morning." Rinsing off her face, Katie turned and kissed Lydia lightly on the lips. "First kiss of the day." Her green eyes sparkled with delight as she wrapped her arms around Lydia's waist.

Lydia smiled. Every morning she kissed Katie while she slept, but had never told her about the ritual. "Always a good beginning." She still felt unnerved by the screams she had heard, but she tried to release her unease and enjoy the moment.

Sharing a few more soft kisses, Lydia drew her fingers over Katie's curls, her diamond ring flashing on her hand.

"The best beginning," Katie decided with a languid sigh. She ran her hand gently over Lydia's cheek to rest against the curve of her neck.

"Did you sleep well?" Lydia could feel her heart calming, her breath slowing. Her usual tranquility was restored as Katie's fingers played with the short dark hair at the nape of her neck.

"Despite all the craziness on the news last night, yes." Katie leaned back against the counter, slowly withdrawing her touch. "Did you?"

"Always, when you're at my side," Lydia answered, speaking the truth. She kissed Katie again, relishing her softness and her warmth.

They fell easily into their regular morning routine. After washing their faces and brushing their teeth, they took hot showers in the massive shower Lydia had especially designed for their home, followed by hair and makeup at their dual vanity before dressing for the day. They chatted about the simple things in their lives: shopping lists, possible movies to rent, attending a party at a friend's house on the weekend.

Lydia loved their early morning chats. Along with her meditation, it grounded her for the rest of the day. As she donned heavy bracelets and an ornate necklace, she watched Katie drag her new high heels out of the closet.

"Trying to impress the judge?"

"He's a leg guy," Katie admitted. She was wearing trousers and a navy silk shell. Her blazer and new cashmere coat were slung over the chair next to the vanity. "Sadly, I have to use my feminine wiles."

"They always work on me," Lydia admitted.

Katie grinned. "Good. Nice to know I've still got it."

"Oh, you've never lost it." Lydia winked.

Sliding on the new shoes, Katie winced. "Ugh! High heels. Ugh!"

"You look lovely. Stop complaining." Lydia took one last look in her floor length mirror. She was wearing a long black silk jersey dress with shiny black boots. The jewelry made the otherwise plain outfit pop with elegance.

Katie mumbled as she walked out of their bedroom toward the kitchen, dragging her stuff with her. Lydia tidied up the vanity, putting away their makeup and hairbrushes, before straightening the golden Buddha sitting on her side. Satisfied, she followed.

When she entered the kitchen, Katie was frowning at her cellphone. "How can I have eight missed calls? Already?"

"Today is court. What do you expect?" Lydia set about whipping up a quick feta and spinach omelet for both of them.

Katie began to listen to the messages as she pulled out some whole grain bread to pop in the toaster. Lydia concentrated on her task, expertly tilting the pan just so, watching the omelet with a skillful eye.

"Weird. It's just a bunch of phone calls asking me if I have watched the news this morning about some riot."

"Probably the same ones as last night. So many unhappy people in the world." Lydia sighed.

Katie slid the phone into her bag. "After the news last night, I really don't want to watch another report on the rioting in Houston. I wonder what the terrorists put in the water to make people act that way?"

"Evil minds come up with evil plots," Lydia answered. "Speaking of evil, your favorite state senator has asked me to decorate her new apartment in downtown Austin. I have an appointment with her today."

Katie hesitated as she got out the orange juice from the refrigerator. "Ugh. No! Paige Brightman? She hates us! She hates gay people!"

"Yes, but I was named the best interior designer in the state in Texas Monthly when they did that cover story on the governor's new house...and she's all about keeping up with the Joneses and keeping appearances."

Katie shook her head. "She has no taste." She poured out some coffee for herself and juice for Lydia.

"She had humble beginnings. Though, I have heard her younger sister is even more of a handful than she is."

"Ugh. That woman! You deliberately didn't tell me!"

"You would have tried to talk me out of it and I think the senator needs a healthy dose of good ol' lesbian hospitality in her life. By the time I'm done decorating her home, she's going to adore me."

Katie continued to make the toast while frowning. "It won't make her fight for our rights, you know. We had to go to Canada to get married."

Lydia nodded. "Exactly. Which is why we should be kind to her."

"You're a much better person than I am," Katie decided with an irritable sigh.

Lydia slid Katie's half of the omelet onto a plate and handed it to her. Carrying her own breakfast, she followed Katie to their breakfast table, snagging the plate of toast on the way.

Dropping the topics of both the disturbing news reports and the senator, they ate breakfast in silence. Katie read from a small Bible her father had given her while eating and sipping orange juice Lydia poured for her. Lydia enjoyed the serenity of the day, watching the sun coming up over the hills. The screams from earlier still haunted her, but she tried not to let them rattle her.

"Still reading the book of Proverbs?" Lydia asked.

"Almost done," Katie answered.

"They're very good meditations," Lydia agreed. "I especially like that verse in Proverbs 5 that says 'may her breasts satisfy you always, may you ever be captivated by her love.'"

Katie almost spit out the coffee she was drinking as Lydia threw back her head and laughed. Looking down at her cleavage, Katie quirked an eyebrow. "So are they satisfying?"

"Oh, yes," Lydia teased.

Grinning, Katie flipped the Bible shut and studied her wife. "You're so bad."

"I'm amazingly good," Lydia corrected.

"I don't want to go to work now! I want to go back to bed!"

"There is always tonight," Lydia promised.

Katie pouted, then noticed the time. "Shit! Gotta run!" Grabbing up her things, she struggled in her high heels, moving toward the front door.

Lydia followed, snagging Katie's laptop bag near the door as they walked out.

"I'll call you when I can, otherwise, I'll text," Katie said as she hurried toward her new convertible, trying not to spill her coffee.

"Remember, we have a late dinner with your father tonight," Lydia said as they reached the car. Katie slung her bag and briefcase behind the driver's seat.

"Right. I got it in my calendar. But before dinner..." Katie grinned wickedly.

"Oh, yes!" Lydia helped Katie into her coat.

A low moan jarred them out of their flirting. They both glanced across their manicured lawn toward their neighbors' house. Through the trees lining the property line they could see David Van Horn staggering around his house, beating his hand against the wall every few steps.

"Poor man," Lydia uttered sympathetically.

"He's drunk again," Katie said with the shake of her head. "Poor Amy. How does she put up with him?"

Reaching the front door of his house, David began to beat on it, moaning loudly.

"Love is a powerful thing. She loves him."

"Even when he's always on benders. Sad." Katie turned to kiss Lydia firmly on the mouth. "Love you."

"I love you," Lydia answered, her fingers lightly trailing over Katie's cheek.

"Tonight," Katie said firmly as she slid behind the wheel, "that whole Proverbs thing."

"I can't wait." Lydia laughed and stepped back as Katie gunned the engine.

As the morning mist wafted around her, slowly dissipating in the rising sun, Lydia waved as Katie pulled her little sports car out of the drive and sped down the road. With a sigh, she crossed her arms and stood on the front lawn listening to the birds calling out to each other and the steady drunken moaning of David next door.

Looking over at the disheveled man, she sighed. She should just go in and clean up after breakfast, but she felt bad for the poor man. Amy was either asleep or ignoring him. Turning on her heel, she headed across the lawn.

"David?" she called out. "David, are you okay?"

Reaching the tall trees separating the lawns, she noticed his car was down the road, smashed into the tree line. Lydia frowned slightly, her eyes glancing toward the man banging on the door.

"David, are you okay? Are you injured?" Maybe he wasn't drunk, but suffering from head trauma.

"David?"

He finally heard her calling and stopped banging on the door. Slowly, he turned. She gasped when she saw the blood staining his face and clothes. His nose was a smashed ruin and his teeth were broken.

"David, oh my God! What happened to you?" Lydia stood with her hand resting against the tree gazing at him in horror.

With an unearthly keening, David lurched toward her, stumbling at a quick pace over the garden his wife so carefully tended.

Lydia began to step toward him, but hesitated. Something was terribly wrong, but she was too stunned to comprehend what was alarming her. David reached out desperately toward her, his fingers grasping.

"Don't let him touch you!" Amy Van Horn stepped out of her house, her fingers trying to staunch the flow of blood pouring from her ravaged left arm. "Don't let him bite you!"

Gasping, Lydia stumbled back from David's outstretched hand. He was within a few feet of her. She turned to flee, but the long skirt of her dress caught in the bushes, making her stumble. He grabbed hold of her shoulder, his fingers cold and hard.

"Don't let him bite you..." Amy sobbed, sounding weaker.

Lydia wrenched her body away from the hand, feeling the cold rasp of his fingers against her skin. He lashed out at her again, making horrible screeching noises. She tried to get her balance and back away from him, but he caught the collar of her dress. Behind him, Amy fell to her knees, weeping, blood spurting from her torn arm. An artery was obviously torn and was pouring her life onto the lawn.

Yanking away from David's clutching hands, Lydia felt the cloth of her dress strain against her skin then began to tear. Her boots slipped on the wet grass, sending her to her knees. Her long fingers clutched at the green grass, her diamond ring glittering in the morning light. Sobbing with fear, she felt tears streaming down her face. She didn't understand what was going on and was utterly terrified.

David fell on her, his heavy body reeking of blood, body odor, and liquor. He scrabbled at her, trying to grab hold of her flailing arms. Flipping onto her back, she fought him, her long nails clawing at his face. His broken teeth snapped at her hands, trying to bite them. Cold, terrible fingers slid over the exposed skin under her bra and for a terrible moment she feared he would rape her. Then his teeth caught the meat of her left hand and he bit down hard.

Screaming, Lydia pummeled the side of his face with her fist. She tried to pull her hand free as he yanked and tugged on her flesh with his teeth. The flashing of her diamond wedding ring blinded her as she struggled. His cold hands sunk into her flesh, forcing her breath from her lungs. Gasping, she tried to get out from under his body and free her hand.

His nails tore at her, pressing harder. The pain was nearly unbearable and she gasped, breathless, unable to pull air into her lungs or free herself from it.

Amy fell to her knees beside them. The sun was behind her, shadowing her face and creating a halo around her red hair.

"Help..." Lydia tried to gasp out. She couldn't breathe. The press of David's hands against her abdomen was unbearable. His nails were cutting her, the pressure and pain building.

Her hand came free from David's mouth with a terrifyingly wet sound. A huge chunk of flesh had been torn free. Lydia reached out to Amy. "Help..."

With a low growl, Amy grabbed her hand and bit into it. David's teeth joined his hands. He tore at her flesh, digging into her stomach. Pain blotted out everything.

It was then she realized she was going to die. That the terrible riots in Houston were something more than anyone had ever imagined and that something evil now roamed the earth. Her blood splashed the faces of her neighbors as they tore into her torso, and she understood that her life was done.

Slightly closing her eyes, she concentrated on her breath, pushing away the pain, pushing away the terror. She managed to get in a small breath and exhale it. She did it again, focusing all her energy on this one simple task. Slowly, she found her center, pushing away the entire world until all that remained was one thought. One word. The word that encompassed her soul, life and world.

"Katie," Lydia whispered, releasing herself to the universe and to her love.

Her neighbors tore her heart from her body, but she was already gone. Her hand slowly fell to her side, the bloodied diamond still sparkling in the morning light.

Monica's Story

Monica De La Torre is an interesting character in the *AS THE WORLD DIES* universe. Her first appearance in the online version of *AS THE WORLD DIES* was as a very minor character working on a construction crew. When I saw her on the movie screen in my mind's eye, I had no idea that she would become an important part of the supporting cast of the series.

I was intrigued by her character and started to explore her relationships with others in the fort. One of her most important relationships is with Juan De La Torre, her cousin. They are very close and regard each other as brother and sister. Later, her relationships with other survivors became a very important plot point in the series.

Sadly, I felt I was never able to explore the past of this very dynamic character in the original online version. When I self-published, I gave Monica a better role and enjoyed her interaction with the other characters. Yet, I was never able to really delve into Monica's past. This short story is my chance to finally give a back story to a really great character.

Monica's original name was Linda, but I realized her name was too similar to Juan's unrequited love, Belinda, and I have changed it for the Tor versions. Her first scene in *AS THE WORLD DIES ZOMBIE TRILOGY* ended up in *FIGHTING TO SURVIVE*, so this short story is a great bridge between the first and second book in the series.

DANGEROUS
HIGHWAYS

Monica hated the taste of gasoline.

She was getting better at siphoning gas from the gas tanks of stranded cars along the highway that sliced through the desert. Unfortunately, this time she waited too long to pull her mouth way from the end of the hose and caught some of the warm, burning fluid in her mouth. Spitting furiously, she grabbed the bottle of water she had placed at her side as a precaution. She quickly rinsed out her mouth while managing to get the end of the hose into the red gas can without spilling too much fuel.

"Shit," she grumbled, then remembered she needed to keep silent.

The dry, hot desert air whipped her ponytail into a frenzy beneath her baseball cap, lashing her face and neck with tendrils of her dark hair. Despite the heat, she was clad in a denim jacket and jeans. Motorcycle gloves and battered cowboy boots completed her outfit. She tried to keep her body as covered as possible not just to fight off the burning rays of the sun or the cool desert air, but also to protect herself from the snapping teeth of the undead.

Crouched down beside a crashed station wagon, she gazed past its crumpled hood wrapped around a utility pole toward the distant mountains. El Paso lay beyond the craggy hills. It had been her home for years, but now it was an undead wasteland. She had barely escaped with her life. If not for Beto's truck, she would have been as dead as her ex-boyfriend.

Scanning the area around her, she shifted on her feet. Her calves were starting to go numb from squatting so long. The gas was flowing like water from a faucet. It made her even thirstier than the mouthful of gasoline. Taking another drag of water, she swished it around her mouth, spit, then took a long drink.

It was eerily quiet along this stretch of Interstate 10. The only noise was the wind, the gasoline filling the can, and the two zombie kids beating on the back window of the station wagon as they growled at her.

Glancing up, she felt a pang of sorrow for the two undead children with dark hair and eyes. They reminded her a little of her and her brother, Sergio, when they had been little. Sadly, both had bites covering their arms and neck. Dressed in cute little Disney outfits caked in dried blood, they were a sad testament to the spread of the plague that had wiped out the world. Their mother was truly dead in the front seat of the wrecked car, her brains splattered across the dashboard and windshield. Their father was nowhere to be seen. He was her real concern. There were no broken windows or open doors. Yet, someone had to have been driving when the crash occurred. She wondered if he had managed to get out of the car and shut the door behind him.

The gas was dying down to a trickle.

The zombie kids beat on the window, smearing it with rot and blood. Morbidly, Monica tapped on the window. Both kids pressed their noses and lips to the glass as they ravenously snapped at her, trying to bite her fingers.

"You're pretty stupid, aren't you?"

Yanking the piece of garden hose she used to siphon the gas free of the car's tank, she stood and scrutinized her surroundings. I-10 was empty except for the station wagon and Beto's big ass monster truck parked behind it. The massive spinners on the side were flecked with blood and gore. Beto's dream car had been her salvation when getting out of El Paso. All the hard work he had done converting an old Ford truck into a monstrous creation with spray-painted flames along its sides, black-painted longhorns fastened to its deer guard, and high suspension had benefited her far more than it had ever impressed his buddies.

Monica trudged over to the monster truck, the gasoline swishing around inside the canister, her hand resting on the pistol tucked into her belt. The weapon was Beto's, too. She had liberated it from his dead hand.

As she climbed up onto the truck bed to refuel, she again searched her surroundings for any sign of the undead. I-10 had been swarming with them after she had escaped the El Paso city limits. The tires were still caked with guts. But this stretch of lonely highway was as empty as the terrain around her.

The zombie children were now beating on a rear window, growling at her hungrily. She stared at them, sighing.

Why was she alive and the kids dead?

In the last year, she had done a lot of things she regretted. Beto was one of those things. A thick limbed, bald, tattooed, cocky Mexican-American, Beto had the allure of a bad boy. A mechanic by trade, with some shady dealings with people on the other side of the border, Beto had considered himself a man to be reckoned with. She had met him while working at Chili's as a waitress of all places. They were together almost a year before she couldn't take his bullshit anymore. He treated her like a princess, but cheated on her constantly.

It was still hard to believe her tough as nails boyfriend was dead while she was still alive. It was his own damn fault he had died. She couldn't believe it was just yesterday that she had been loading the last of her possessions into her old beat-up Mustang while Beto yelled at her. She now wondered if it had been his loud proclamations of his love and the insignificance of his affairs which had drawn attention to him. Banging the trunk shut, she straightened ready to tell him off when she saw a nightmarish creature racing across the street toward Beto.

Monica's first thought was that the man with the mangled face had to be playing a joke. Zombies didn't exist, yet her gut told her what she was seeing was real. When she finally managed to scream a warning, it had been too late. The zombie slammed into Beto, its jagged teeth tearing into his meaty neck.

Beto had instinctively drawn his gun, but it was too late. A steady diet of medical dramas had educated Monica enough for her to know that the zombie had hit an artery. The arc of blood had been a fountain that splashed over the zombie and Monica. As Beto fell, she had kicked the zombie in the face with her booted heel. Intent on its prey, it had ignored her. Snatching up the gun from Beto's still quivering hand, she had stood over the creature and Beto. Two bullets into the back of the zombie's head stilled it. Sobbing, she had scanned her surroundings as she stood over her boyfriend as his death throes ebbed away.

"Fuck," she whispered, wiping his blood from her face. If Juan's stupid zombie movies were right, Beto would come back. Yet, she hesitated. She couldn't bring herself to shoot him. Maybe he wouldn't turn into a zombie.

When Beto's dead eyes opened and he let out an unearthly howl, she shot him twice in the head.

"Fuck, it's really zombies," she gasped.

Terrified, she grabbed her suitcases out of the back of her Mustang and tossed them into the bed of Beto's truck, grabbed his keys, and hauled ass. Driving like a mad woman through the outskirts of El Paso, she had seen things looked like scenes out of those stupid movies her cousin Juan was always watching. Yet, she had to be grateful for his obsession for it had saved her life. She had known exactly how to kill both Beto and the zombie.

Unscrewing the cap off the gas tank of the monster truck, Monica tried not to dwell on the terrible events of the preceding day. Every time she thought about the moment when she saw that first zombie, her hands started to shake. With trembling fingers she shoved the gas can nozzle into place, pouring the fuel into the truck. The gas chugged into the almost dry tank as she leaned over the edge of the truck bed. Her hair beat against her sunglasses as she prayed the gas would last until she could find more to siphon.

Glancing back down the highway, she wondered if Juarez was still burning and if El Paso was in flames yet. During her crazy escape out of the city, she had seen the fires burning on the other side of the border.

Turning her gaze in the opposite direction, she wondered how long it would take her to get to her home town. Ashley Oaks, Texas was far away. It had been difficult getting this far, maneuvering through the crowded, zombie infested highway, then off-roading it for miles as she tried to avoid the massive traffic jams. She had spent the night hunkered down in the cab of the truck, listening to explosions in the distance.

"God, I'm hungry," she muttered.

She would need food soon. Water too.

Sweat trickled down her nose, and she wiped her face with her gloved hand. She had to believe her family in Ashley Oaks was still alive. Though her brother Sergio wasn't always the smartest guy when it came to choosing his friends, he could handle himself pretty well. Hopefully, her *Tia* Rosie was safe with Juan. Her own *mama* and *papa* were long dead in a tragic car accident. Rosie, Juan and Sergio were all she had left in the world. She had to believe they were safe in Ashley Oaks. Now she just needed to get there.

She was screwing the cap back onto the gas tank when she heard something impact against the side of the truck. Her heart lurching with fear, she whipped about, drawing her weapon.

"Help me!"

Slowly, she stepped toward the other side of the truck that faced the road and peered over the edge of the truck bed. A man was leaning heavily against the door, his hand beating against the metal. His hair was full of dust and his face was badly sunburned.

Swollen eyes tried to focus on her as his chapped lips parted to speak.

"Help me!"

"Are you bitten?"

Shaking his head, the man dragged in deep breaths of air. Sweat poured down the sides of his face and his clothes were damp.

"No, ma'am," he said. "You have to help me."

The zombie kids snarled and beat their fists against the back window of the station wagon, their dead eyes fixed on the man.

"Where were you?" Monica looked around at the barren landscape again.

"Hiding in a ditch up the road. I woke up and saw your truck."

"What is your name?"

"Ramon."

"Is that your car, Ramon?"

With a sob, the man nodded. "Yes. We got out of El Paso, but my wife was bitten when she escaped from her job. She was lying in the back with the kids. I thought she was asleep, but then the kids started screaming. She...she...was...." He covered his face with his hand, trying not to look at the station wagon and its terrible passengers. "She was attacking the kids. I...I...she came for me, too, and the car swerved and she..."

"You don't have to finish. I get it," Monica said. It wasn't too hard to put the pieces together. The zombie wife attacked him, he jerked the wheel, hit the pole, the zombie wife hurtled into the dashboard bashing her brains out, and Ramon escaped the car.

"Please, help me," Ramon whispered. "Please."

Tucking her gun into her jeans, Monica lowered herself over the side of the truck. Her feet were almost to the ground when she felt Roman yank the gun away.

"What the hell?" she roared at him, landing with a heavy thud on the highway.

"Give me the keys," Ramon ordered. His hand was shaking and his dark eyes were dangerous with grief and a deeper, more terrible emotion.

"No way," Monica answered her anger building. "You're trying to jack my truck after I was going to help you?"

"I need to get out of here!" Ramon shouted, spittle flying from his cracked lips. "I can't stand it here! They're all dead!"

"Dude, I will take you with me if you calm the fuck down!"

"I have to get out of here!" Ramon screamed. "I have to get out of here! Don't you understand?"

The zombie kids were in a frenzy now.

"I am not giving you my truck!"

Ramon pointed the gun at her chest. "Give me the keys!"

"Why are you doing this?"

"I have to get out of here!"

It was the intensity in his eyes and the desperation in his voice that finally drove home the fact that the man had lost his mind. He was beyond reason. His body violently shaking, he winced every time he heard the dead children slam their hands against the window.

Lowering her voice, Monica said, "Ramon, let me take you away from here." There was no way in hell she had survived this long to let a crazy person steal her transportation.

"I knew she was dead, but I kept driving," he whispered. "I kept driving because I was afraid."

Monica swallowed hard, fighting to keep her emotions and words in check. She was so angry it was pushing her fear away and she couldn't afford to be stupid with a gun pointed at her chest.

"I thought maybe she wouldn't come back like the others. It was such a small bite. More like a scratch. The kids were crying, telling me she wouldn't wake up, but I kept driving. Even when they started to scream, I just kept driving."

Monica realized Ramon wasn't talking to her. His confession was for himself and maybe his kids. She could see his eyes struggling not to stray in the direction of the children.

"Ramon, we all make mistakes," she said at last.

"I need to get away from here," Ramon mumbled again.

"Where are you going to go, Ramon?"

"I don't know. Somewhere…"

"Let me take you with me to my cousin's place. He's a big zombie freak. He'll know what to do." Monica's gaze did not waver from the weapon.

Ramon shook his head, tears falling down his burnt cheeks as snot dribbled from his nose. "No, no. There is no hope."

"Ramon, let's work together. We have to stick together. We're still alive," Monica insisted.

"You're not my fucking friend, bitch! You're not my family! My family is dead!" Ramon howled at her, his finger starting to pull the trigger.

Monica dove to one side and grabbed his arm as momentum carried her past him. The gun did not fly out of his hand as she had hoped. Instead, he began to fire the weapon as he fell. The bullets punched into the side of the vehicle. Ramon landed on his back and immediately started to swing the weapon toward her. Monica lunged over his chest and grabbed his wrist, pushing it away with her body weight.

Ramon continued to fire.

Glass shattered near them as they fought on the ground for the weapon. Deranged and beyond reason, Ramon screamed wordlessly at her.

The gun clicked empty.

Driving her elbow into Ramon's nose, Monica scrambled backward. She knew what the sound of the breaking glass meant. Fumbling for her keys, she dared to look toward the back of the station wagon. The little girl was already on the ground, crawling toward her father. The little boy was worming his way through the hole in the window. Ramon lay on the ground, sobbing and blubbering as he watched his dead children approach.

Monica swore under her breath. Pulling the door open, she climbed into the driver's seat and twisted the key in the ignition. The big truck roared to life and she quickly shifted gears. Backing the truck up, she saw Ramon reaching out to embrace his zombified children.

Pressing her lips into a grim line, Monica drove around the man leaving him to his fate.

Her fate lay elsewhere.

Eric's Story

Eric was one of the characters swept to one side by my busy schedule and crazy writing spurts when I originally wrote *AS THE WORLD DIES* online. Though I always saw him in my mind's eye as a valuable part of the fort and adored his character, he always seemed to end up just off screen. Just before self-publishing the first book in the series, *THE FIRST DAYS*, in August 2008, I wrote *Eric's Story* online for the fandom to enjoy while waiting for the sequels to be published.

I was surprised when the novella gained its own following. People who had not read the original series found the story and loved it. Because of the outpouring of love for Eric and his little dog, Pepe, I was happy to have the chance to integrate the characters into the revised versions of the trilogy.

I have decided to dust off, polish up, and reissue *Eric's Story* since it is a perfect bridge between *THE FIRST DAYS* and second book of the series, *FIGHTING TO SURVIVE*.

The Vacation of the Undead

1.
All is Calm

Eric's eyelids slowly fluttered open as the full force of the morning sun struck his face. With a slow, painful moan, he turned his head away from the bright beam of sunlight reflecting off the stained glass borders of the tall bedroom windows. Evidently the sun had been cooking his left arm for a few minutes. It felt hot as he laid it across his chest to get it out of the sun. He had lost all feeling in his right arm. Brandy was laying on top of it in all her tanned, smooth-skinned glory. Her streaked blond hair was hanging over her face and she had shoved the covers off both of them in her sleep. She was naked, gorgeous and snoring loudly.

It took some work to get her off his arm. He had to shove her a few times to get her to move. She thrashed a little, striking his chin with one elbow before rolling over and continuing her snores. Struggling to sit up, he rubbed his arm and looked at the digital clock on the antique bed stand next to the four poster bed. It was nearly eleven o'clock in the morning.

His movements reminded him of how much wine he had consumed the night before and his vision swam as his brain quivered in his skull. The annoying wine hangover was in full force.

Leaning over, he managed to find his boxers in the heap of clothes next to the bed and pull them on. His legs were the pale, skinny, hairy opposite of Brandy's incredible limbs. But then again, he slogged away in an office ten hours a day while she jogged and played tennis between her modeling jobs. It still amazed him that he was dating such an amazingly beautiful woman when he was a tall, gawky, average looking guy.

Scratching his thigh as he walked to the bathroom, he noted the three bottles of wine strewn next to the bed and the remains of their gourmet meal tucked away on a silver tray next to the door. The bed and breakfast wouldn't tidy up until they left for the day or set the tray outside the door. He opened the door and shoved the tray out with one foot and then added the wine bottles.

Behind him, Brandy snored on.

Outside the birds sang and the wind rustled the limbs of the huge pecan trees hovering over the reconstructed farmhouse. It was a comforting sound. He took a moment to look out the window into the garden and saw it was empty save for a cat gingerly making its way across the stone walkway.

The shower was hot and refreshing and he was amazed at how sore he felt. But then again, it had been a sexual marathon the likes he had never done before. After weeks of working on a major project, he had finally had the chance to take time off and spend it with Brandy. It was obvious he had been neglecting her in a certain area and she had been demanding and exciting. As he soaped up his rather shabby chest, he once more vowed to work out and get into shape. Luckily, his clothes hid his slowly expanding stomach and still gave the impression of him being lean and long, but that would only last for so long before he headed into the uncomfortable world of being overweight. His head throbbed from the wine as he washed his medium brown hair that so perfectly matched his medium brown eyes. Everything about him was just medium, except for his girlfriend. She was exceptional.

Most of his friends hated her, but he was sure that they were just jealous. They complained she was spoiled and he knew, guiltily, that this was true. He always bought her the best of everything, from her car to her clothes. She kept their home immaculate and always made him feel wonderful. They did occasionally have fierce battles, but mostly because he was still uncomfortable with his growing wealth and she was not. He still tended to keep a penny jar and buy his clothes at JC Penny.

Dressing in Dockers and a button down shirt (but he did roll up the sleeves and unbutton the collar), he stood in front of the misty mirror in the bathroom and took a deep breath.

Today was the day.

He was going to ask her to marry him. He had been carrying around a 4-carat diamond (she had told him from day one she would settle for nothing less) for weeks now and last night he had chickened out. Or perhaps had just been distracted by her throwing off her clothes. Either way, he had not pulled out the little blue box with the diamond ring inside.

"Okay, Eric, today. Today you're going to do it." He put on his glasses, nodded to his reflection, and walked out into the bedroom.

Brandy was still asleep, snoring, and now had one long leg dangling off the bed.

"When she wakes up," he murmured, and let himself out of their room.

The hall and stairway were empty as he hurried down to the kitchen. The proprietor of the bed and breakfast, a woman in her early forties with masses of red hair, was completely absorbed in the small TV resting on the counter and jumped when he touched her arm.

"Oh, Mr. Hertzenburger, you gave me a start!"

"I'm so sorry, Mrs. Waskom. I just wanted to see if I could get brunch for me and my girlfriend?"

Mrs. Waskom nodded as her gaze slid back to the TV. "Of course. I can have it set up for you in the dining room unless you want to eat in your room or on the patio?"

Eric glanced toward the TV and saw a scene of mayhem. "Is that Iraq?"

"No," Mrs. Waskom answered. "It's Chicago."

The TV screen was filled with the view of a smoke covered street. Bloodied figures were stumbling through falling debris as a large building crumbled slowly into the crowd.

"Oh, God," Eric gasped.

"A plane crashed," Mrs. Waskom explained. "It just went down into a neighborhood."

"Terrorists?" Eric swallowed hard.

"They're not saying," the woman answered and wiped a tear away.

Blackened figures stumbled toward the news reporter while she delivered her solemn take on the scene. Fire trucks continued to arrive behind her as the charred victims staggered toward the arriving rescuers. It was horrifying to behold.

"Eric," Brandy's voice whined behind him.

He quickly turned to find her standing in the hallway, her silk robe wrapped around her firm body. Her long hair framed her face in a sexy mess as she pouted at him.

"Brandy, I was getting us brunch."

"I woke up and you weren't there," she said grumpily.

"I'm sorry, baby." He rushed toward her, then stopped and quickly said to the distracted owner. "Brunch on the patio will be perfect."

Mrs. Waskom again started at the sound of his voice, then nodded. Flipping off the TV, she moved deeper into the kitchen. "It will be out in fifteen minutes."

Brandy tugged at his belt and looked up at him through her thick lashes. "I don't like it when you just leave me."

"I'm sorry, honey. I am. Why don't you get dressed and we'll have brunch?"

Her lips were soft against his and she snuggled into his side. "Okay. But no more TV. You promised me I would have you all to myself."

"Okay. No more TV," he vowed.

2.
Not Quite Right

"You said that you weren't going to ignore me," Brandy exclaimed as they entered their room. She spun about on her bare heel to glare at him.

"I'm not, honey. I was arranging for us to eat. The TV was on and-"

"Eric, you said no TV. No phone calls. No gaming. That is what you said."

"The cell phone is off, I didn't even bring my computer, and the TV in here is unplugged. I swear. This time is only about you." He was eager to placate her so the argument would die quickly.

At times her anger at him for his perceived inattention to her was a bit frightening. She had once deleted his primary World of Warcraft character after he had played all evening. In one fell swoop, he lost two years of endless grinding, raiding, questing, and all the gear he had obtained. It had been a huge blow, but as she sobbed at his computer that he didn't love her as much as he loved the game, he understood that she needed to know he loved her more than anything else in his life. That was when he bought her a new car and swore off gaming except for one night a week.

She sniffled a little and swept her hair back from her face. Her eyes were hazel and sometimes looked like amber, and the thick lashes made her eyes sultry and intense. Her long brown hair had huge streaks of blond through it and its very expensive cut made it look amazing no matter how long she had slept on it. The smattering of light freckles on her turned-up nose made her adorable.

Taking her in his arms, he kissed her lips and said, "This is all about you. I promise."

"Okay," she said with a little smile. "I forgive you."

He kissed her again and held her close. "Why don't you take a shower and I'll go get Pepe and take him for a walk. We can meet out on the patio for brunch."

She slid from his arms and sauntered toward the bathroom. "Make sure he doesn't smell."

"I promise," Eric answered, let himself out of the room, and hurried down the stairs to the front door.

The main draw to the Crystal Waters Farm and Bed and Breakfast had been that they allowed guests to bring their pets. For an additional fee, there was an onsite kennel so that visitors could enjoy their vacation and not have to leave their furry little companion at home. Eric strode through the gardens and out the gate toward the old barn that loomed nearby. Next to it was a small building that housed the visiting pets.

Gloria, a petite Latina with sleek blond hair and dark brown eyes, greeted him when he entered the building. There were four kennels for the four available suites in the bed and breakfast and Pepe was the only dog visiting. The small Jack Russell terrier instantly jumped to his feet and ran to the door, his tail wagging.

"Has he been okay?"

"A perfect angel," Gloria answered, smiling down at the little dog. "I took him for a walk earlier and he was very excited to see the squirrels."

"That's my boy," Eric said with a grin. "A rough and tough hunter of vermin."

Gloria swung open the door and the tiny dog leaped into his arms. Eric was quickly covered in dog saliva as he received the messiest of dog kisses, but he laughed and held the dog lovingly.

"I'm going to take him out for awhile and bring him back in a few hours," Eric said.

"I work around the barn area, so just give me a call," Gloria answered.

"I was wondering if-"

Gloria's cell phone rang. For a moment Eric almost checked his own phone, and then remembered it was in the glove compartment of the car.

"I need to take this," she said with a smile, turning away. "Yeah, Joshua? I told you not to call me at work unless it was an emergency. What is it?"

Eric hesitated, then started toward the door.

"What did Grandma say? Why would Mr. Sanchez be trying to eat Grandpa? Joshua, something else must be wrong. Did you tell her to call the police or an ambulance?"

Eric glanced toward the woman as he began to step outside. The phone call was odd and it was hard not to want to hear the end of it.

"Look, Joshua, Mr. Sanchez is a diabetic. If he didn't take his medicine, he might be having some sort of fit. You need to call Grandma and tell her to call the ambulance and the police. We're nowhere near San Antonio. We can't do anything. You're sixteen years old. You can handle calling her. Now don't bother me at work anymore. Use your head." Gloria hung up and noticed Eric lingering. "My mother has dementia. She calls my house all the time with wild stories."

"That was some story," Eric said with a laugh.

Gloria nodded and rolled her eyes. "Dad won't put her in a nursing home, so we have to put up with some weird stuff."

"Gotcha. Well, thanks for taking care of Pepe."

"No problem. He's a sweetheart." Gloria leaned down to pet Pepe's little head.

The dog licked her hand then trotted to the end of his leash and looked back at Eric expectantly.

"I better go. See you later."

Stepping outside, Eric admired the brilliant blue sky full of billowing clouds and breathed in the fresh scent of the spring air. The world was blooming again and the nearby peach trees were stunning with purple and lavender flowers. It was a perfect April morning.

Well, almost afternoon.

Behind him, he heard Gloria's cell phone begin to ring again. Then another phone began to ring faintly in the distance. Curious, Eric turned to see a man in a cowboy hat fishing his phone out of his jeans as he led a horse toward the stable. Then, even fainter, another phone began to ring.

Eric shifted uncomfortably on his feet, unnerved for some inexplicable reason.

Pepe let out a little *arf* to get him moving and they began to walk as the third cell phone continued to ring for a few seconds before it was also picked up.

The wind picked up the cowboy's voice and Eric heard him say, "Then call the police, honey. I can't do nothing from here. Look, if some bum is trying to get into the neighbor's house, call the cops. Get the shotgun out of the closet and if he bothers you, remember don't shoot until he's in the house. Now hang up, call the cops, and then call me back."

Pepe gripped the cuff of Eric's pants in his teeth and yanked on him a few times.

"Okay, okay. Walk time. Sheesh," Eric said to the little dog.

Together they started down the path.

Somewhere, in the distance, another phone began to ring.

3.
The World Begins To End

There was the distinct feeling of unease despite the bright sunlight, cool breeze, and beautiful surroundings. After brunch, Eric and Brandy had loaded Pepe into the car and driven down to the quaint Texan town nestled below the hill the B & B rested on. After parking and making sure Pepe's leash was secure, they set out for a long nice walk while window shopping in the restored downtown.

His credit cards were hurting from Brandy's shopping spree the day before so they mostly gazed in the windows at the opulent displays and let Pepe explore. Every crack in the sidewalk seemed to entice the little dog.

Brandy had settled down after their brunch and was sweetly smiling. It was a huge relief to Eric and he tried hard not to disrupt the pleasantness of the day. But still, he was greatly bothered by the feeling that something terrible was happening somewhere out in the world. He hated not having access to the news.

To Eric, the walk was far from relaxed. Brandy seemed oblivious of the tense expressions on the faces of the locals or the noticeable lack of tourists. It was a weekday and the busy shopping days were the weekends, but Eric noticed quite a few touristy looking types hurrying to their cars. The groups of pedestrians on Main Street were thinning significantly as more and more people received calls on their cell phones that prompted them to rush off.

"Things seem...'off' today," he finally ventured.

Brandy looked at him blankly. "What do you mean?"

"People. They seem off."

Brandy rolled her eyes. "It's because you can't get onto the computer or check in with work."

"That plane crash in Chicago was a little scary. Maybe that's it. Maybe it feels too much like 9/11."

"Gawd. I wish people would get over that," Brandy sniffed. "It was a long time ago. People need to let it go."

"Brandy," Eric chided her gently, "that event changed our world."

Brandy scoffed at this. "Yeah, like it didn't take forever at the airport before."

"You do remember the war, right?"

"It's not a war. It's nation building," Brandy said firmly. "Daddy explained it to me."

Eric tried not to sound sarcastic, but he couldn't help but say, "Yeah. Mr. Staunch Republican."

"Daddy is just older and wiser than you. He says it's
natural for young men to be more liberal because you
haven't gained wisdom yet."

Eric felt Pepe nudge his ankle and looked down at the
small dog. The dog regarded him with a somber expression
and licked his muzzle. Feeling the need to change the
subject, he said, "I think Pepe is thirsty."

"He also smells. He was rolling in something again."
Brandy sighed.

Pepe had been a gift for Brandy. When she had asked for
a "small dog", he hadn't realized she wanted a teacup
Chihuahua. The lack of her clarity on the subject had
resulted in him proudly presenting the Jack Russell Terrier
and her declaring, "He's so not fitting in my purse." Pepe
had instantly ended up being his dog and Brandy lost
interest in the whole concept of having a little furry thing to
tuck into her fashionable purses. Sometimes Brandy was
quite affectionate to Pepe, but she quickly lost interest if he
did anything too overtly dog-like.

"Look, there's a gas station on the corner. We'll stop
there, I'll grab him some water and a Diet Coke for you," Eric
said as he began to move on down the sun baked sidewalk.

"Well, okay," Brandy said, and reluctantly tore her gaze
away from a dress in a window.

Anticipating a nice cold drink, Pepe scampered ahead,
tugging insistently on his leash and making Eric hurry. They
reached the quaint, old fashioned gas station ahead of
Brandy, and Eric looked back to check on her progress. She
was sauntering along with her usual sexy model walk, her
hair shining in the sunlight, and her tanned limbs glistening
with a sheen of perspiration. He smiled realizing again how
helplessly in love he was with her.

The door to the building opened and a bell jingled merrily
overhead as a pale faced man and frightened looking woman
hurried out followed by three 'tween boys.

"Hurry, we got to go now!" The father grabbed the
youngest boy's hand and yanked him along as the mother
tried to run in her kitten-heeled flip-flops. The tiny narrow

heels hitting the cement made a sharp sound, and Pepe barked at her.

Eric watched in bewilderment as the family piled into a SUV and tore out of the lot and almost hit another car as it tried to get onto Main Street.

"What a total ass," Brandy scowled, and flipping her hair over one shoulder.

"That was weird. Here. Watch Pepe and I'll get our stuff." He handed over the leash quickly before she could protest. He was quite anxious now to find out what had everyone so rattled. If Brandy stayed outside, he could possibly get some news while inside the gas station.

Brandy sniffed the air over the dog and Pepe looked up at her with what Eric could swear was an annoyed look. "He needs a bath. They need to bathe him tonight."

"Okay, I'll order one for him. I'll be right back." He kissed her cheek and quickly moved inside.

The bell jingled over his head as Eric entered and he saw a tall, thin man standing behind the counter watching the news on a small TV tucked up on a shelf. The interior store was set up like an old general store and the wood floor creaked under his feet as he hurriedly grabbed what he needed. Eric could barely hear the voice of the news commentator over the sound of the old freezers kicking on.

"...as the fire spreads through that area of Chicago we are receiving continuous reports of mass looting, violence, and possible murders. The National Guard has been called in to quell the violence and we still have no report of what happened to the first emergency crews to arrive at the crash site..."

Eric moved up to the counter and looked toward the TV to see scenes of fire and mayhem being played out as the commentator's voice droned on.

"The shocking video of our own reporter, Trish Kendrick, will be shown again in ten minutes. We warn you that the footage is disturbing. Based on the brutality of the attack we believe that Trish and her cameraman, Arnold Franco, are deceased. The footage shows an attack similar to ones being reported in Chicago and in several other cities."

"Was it terrorists?" Eric's voice cracked and he felt sick to his stomach seeing the footage.

"Dunno," the older man answered. "They're trying to figure it out. Said that some girl on the plane was attacking other people and they strapped her down. That was the last thing the air traffic controller heard before it crashed. Got some other riots going down in some other cities." The man began to ring up his purchases, carefully entering the prices into an ancient cash register by punching down the big black keys.

"Is that why everyone is acting so odd?" Eric cast a wary glance toward Brandy outside. He was surprised to see her playing with Pepe.

"Not paying attention to the news, huh?"

"Well, we're on a little romantic vacation, so not really."

"People are freaking out. Think its terrorists putting something in the water or in the air. Rioting in some of the big cities up North. Army and National Guard will get it under control. Some weird stuff going on today, that's for sure. Newspeople can't decide what's going on. They say terrorists, then they say race riots." The man shrugged. "They're probably making it a bigger deal than it is."

"I hope so. How much do I owe you?"

"Four dollars and fifty-two cents." He rested his huge hands on the counter to lean toward him. "You know, its time like this, I'm glad I'm in Texas. We got guns and balls, son."

"That we do," Eric answered with a chuckle, handing over the exact change.

"Take care," the man said.

"You, too," Eric answered, and headed back outside.

Brandy stood in the sun, probably trying to get a better tan, while Pepe dug into a flowerbed nestled against the side of the gas station. In some ways he felt relieved knowing that whatever was happening was far away, but at the same time he didn't like a terrorist attack occurring on American soil.

Briefly, he felt a twinge of terror skitter through his brain. He shoved it away into the back of his thoughts. Things would be fine. Chicago was far away and this was a time to enjoy with his girlfriend and his beloved dog.

It was a struggle, but he managed to ignore his nagging fear and enjoy the rest of his day and evening. When he finally fell into bed that night, he felt content and loved. With Brandy nestled in his arms, he felt confident that everything was going to be just fine. Tomorrow, he would give her the ring and it would be perfect.

At 3 AM he found out how wrong he was...

4.
The Morning of the Last Day

Eric woke from a very deep sleep and wasn't immediately sure why. The bed was deliciously warm compared the coldness filling the room and he drowsily raised his head to look at the clock next to the bed. The big red numbers read 3:00. Blinking, he slowly reached out to touch Brandy. His hand slid over the covers to find she was not there. It was then that he became aware of her voice speaking in a hushed voice.

Sliding out of the bed, he stood for a second trying to figure out where she was in the dark. Slowly, he realized she was not in the room at all, but the bathroom. Confused as to whom she could possibly be talking to, he moved toward the door, tilting his head to hear. As his awakening mind grew sharper, so did his hearing.

"...cannot believe you went out with my sister. No, I haven't told him, but I already told you I'm not sure what is going on between us. I thought I knew, but this time with Eric has been so good. Oh, fuck you. No, fuck you. You took my sister out and got her attacked! You're at the fucking hospital with my sister. Do not tell me to calm down," Brandy's voice was whispering harshly.

Eric felt an intense, cold shiver run through his body and his stomach rolled. He raised his hand to knock on the door, but he just couldn't bear to. Instead, he laid his palm against the door and listened.

"Just tell me if she's going to be okay. Paul, a fucking bum bit the hell out of her neck and you're telling me to calm down? You fucking asshole. I can't believe I slept with you. I can't believe I was going to leave Eric for you. No, I don't feel bad that the bum bit you, too. No. No. It's over. No, it's definitely over. You know how much my sister means to me. You fucking know it and you take her out on a date!" Her voice was growing louder. She realized it and caught herself. Her voice was much lower when she said, "You sleep with her and I'll fucking cut your dick off."

Feeling numb, Eric turned and staggered back to the bed. Unable to completely absorb the overhead conversation or believe it, he pulled the covers over him and lay there staring at the clock. It read 3:02.

In just two minutes, everything had changed.

At her request, he had left his cell phone in the car, but she must have hidden hers in her makeup case. And while he had staunchly avoided all calls, she was on the phone with Paul, her womanizing friend that Eric had never liked. Not only on the phone, but ragging on him for taking her sister, Rachel, out. That would have been understandable considering Paul's reputation, but to hear that she had cheated on him with that bastard was too much for Eric to bear. He closed his eyes, tears spilling around his lashes.

It was a nightmare and he just wanted to sleep. In the morning it would be okay. It would all be a nightmare. But his mind would not let him sleep, and he could feel his heart pounding hard in his chest.

A few minutes later Brandy crawled into bed and snuggled up to his back. He could feel the tension in her body and he tried not to shirk from her touch. He remained still, pretending he was asleep, but she was soon thrashing around irritably, trying to get comfortable.

Sleep never came back to him. He watched the minutes on the clock changing, then the hours. Brandy kept tossing and turning and crawled out of bed a few times to go to the bathroom. Each time, he heard her lowered voice as she spoke on the phone. After the calls, she would return to bed to fidget even more.

Finally, the sun began to filter through the stained glass bordering the windows after seven o'clock. Brandy slid out of bed again and went to the bathroom. When the door shut softly behind her, he sat up and swung his legs over the edge of the bed.

All night he had been tormented by the thought of her cheating on him. Without a doubt, he knew he loved her. He just didn't know what to do. He needed to have her explain to him, ask for forgiveness, anything to make it better. After four hours of sheer torture, he was ready to talk.

"What the hell are you saying? From a bite? My sister did not die from a bite! You're a fucking liar! I don't care if you're not feeling good. You're telling me my sister died? You're lying! You're lying!"

The bathroom door slammed open and Brandy stumbled out. She didn't even hide her phone smashed up against her ear. She plugged in the TV and hit the button to turn it on not even noticing Eric standing nearby.

"I don't understand. What do you mean? Why are you lying to me, Paul? What's on TV?"

Brandy hit the buttons to change the channel. Suddenly the TV screen was full of images of bloodied people storming through a city street. They were attacking everyone in sight and the police were firing into the crowd. Eric felt his stomach twist hard as he saw the Texas Capital building in the background and realized the chaos was on Congress Street in Austin. Their home was in turmoil.

"Fuck you, Paul. I'm coming right now to take care of my sister." Brandy hung up and ran to the closet to pull out her luggage.

"Are you seeing this?" Eric finally spoke.

"We're going back," Brandy answered firmly, her long streaked hair swinging around her face as she shoved her clothes into the suitcase.

"Are you seeing what is going on in Austin?" Eric looked back at the screen.   He scowled as the reporter's voice droned on. National Guard soldiers were shooting into a rabid mass of people who were trying to attack them.

"The army is there. They'll fix it by the time I get there. Rachel is in the hospital. Some bum bit her last night and she's sick," Brandy said. "Mom and Dad are in France, and I need to be there."

"Brandy, are you actually paying attention to the news? We can't go back," Eric said in a voice that sounded strangely calm despite the trembling of his hands.

As she pulled on a pair of shorts, she glared at him. "Don't tell me what to do. The army is there. Get your stuff. We're going now!"

Eric reluctantly began to pull on his Dockers from the day before. The local Texas news cut to the national feed. A map of the United States appeared with red dots surrounding several major cities. He sat down hard on the bed in shock as the ticker at the bottom of the screen told of the growing violence in the cities. He reached over and snagged the remote and turned up the sound.

"... continues as normal in some parts of the country this morning as growing violence develops in several cities. The government has issued a statement that all the violence has been isolated only to certain areas and that people should continue on with their normal schedules. The violence in Austin, Texas this morning is being reported as the result of drunken rowdiness after a secret rave at a downtown nightclub. The National Guard has the situation under control. We are being told it is not associated in any way with the race riots in New York, Detroit and Philadelphia nor the suspected terrorism in Chicago yesterday..." a very calm reporter droned on while the scenes of violence played out behind her.

"They're lying. This much rioting happening all at once? And look at those scenes. People are biting each other!" Eric's voice sounded odd to his ears. Too high pitched. And his stomach rolled once more.

"We're going. They said it's under control. My sister is in the hospital and her drugged out buddy is being a shithead."

"You mean the guy you slept with?" The words slipped out before he could stop them.

Brandy was heaving her heavy suitcase off a chair. She hesitated at his words. "Fuck you."

"Well, evidently you're fucking someone else," Eric said defensively.

"My sister is in the hospital, dickwad!" She threw his shoes at him and his shirt from the day before. "If you love me, you'll come with me."

"Brandy, are you even watching the news? Something is wrong. They put PCP in the water or something. Or some kind of chemical."

"Who?"

"Terrorists or something," Eric said. "Don't you see what is going on? Look at where the red dots are. They're around major cities. Being in a major city is a danger right now. Your sister is in the hospital and that's a safe place to be. We need to stay here until they figure out what the hell is going on!"

Brandy's lips set in a tight line, she shoved past him, and barged out the door.

"Brandy, don't!"

Eric shoved his shoes on as fast as he could and ran out after her. Pulling his shirt on, he rushed down the stars as she dragged her suitcase down the stairs.

"You can't tell me not to go be with her. If you love me you'll go with me and stop being a jerk."

Brandy yanked the front door open and charged outside.

"Brandy, listen to me, honey. People are attacking each other, biting each other, they're rioting. You can't go back to Austin until they tell us for sure it's over."

"The news said it was under control. I'm going to be with my sister and punch Paul in the face," Brandy snapped, barely glancing over her shoulder at him.

"Why? Because he's trying to sleep with your sister, too?"

"You were listening to my phone calls?" Brandy whirled around, her eyes burning bright with anger and her lips set into a tight line.

"Yeah, I overheard you." Eric felt his rage fill him once more, but then it burst inside of him and he felt a sob in his throat. "But I love you and I don't care. We'll get counseling. We can work through this. I've been working too much, neglecting you."

Brandy stared at him for a few seconds then turned around and continued her march toward the car. "Then if you love me, you'll come with me."

Eric hurried after her. "Brandy, listen to me, sweetheart. I think if we go back we might die. Do you understand? We stand a good chance of getting killed. Those red dots are over the cities, Brandy. Don't you understand? The more people there are the more dangerous whatever this thing is becomes."

His girlfriend shoved her suitcase into the back of the car and once more turned to face him. "If you love me, you will come with me."

Tears were threatening as he reached out and touched her cheek gently. She slightly turned her head away from him and it hurt him. "Okay."

"Good." She pulled the driver side door open, leaned over, and pulled out the small black case they kept their revolver in. They never traveled without it. "We've got this. We'll be fine. Let's go."

Eric wiped a tear away and felt his nose quivering. He felt overwhelmed and afraid. But somehow, through the chaotic swirl of his thoughts he heard Pepe's tiny yap. The little dog was in the fenced in yard of the kennel and had heard their voices.

"Okay, but I need to get Pepe."

"Leave him," Brandy said in a cold voice.

"I can't," Eric protested.

"We can come back for him, but right now we've got to go! We can't waste time dropping him off at home. My sister is in the fucking hospital, Eric!"

"And she's dead, Brandy. Isn't that what Paul said?" He regretted the words the minute he said them.

Brandy's face flushed red. "No, she's not and if you love me, you'll get in this gawddamn car right now!"

Eric gripped the edge of the car door while struggling with his emotions. "I'll get Pepe, then we'll go."

"Leave the dog, Eric."

"No, I can't. I'll get him and be right back."

This one thing he could not do for her. He would not leave Pepe behind. He sprinted down the path away from the house and the covered parking lot toward the kennel just beyond the garden. He ran as fast as he could, tears slipping down his cheeks. Brandy and Pepe were everything to him and he would not lose either one of them. Somehow, this all had to work out.

The kennel came into view. Pepe was standing on his hind feet, his front paws resting on the fence as he barked anxiously. Eric rushed to the gate in the enclosure and fumbled with the latch until it opened. Pepe immediately ran and jumped into his arms. The feel of the warm, anxious little body in his arms soothed his shattered nerves a tad. He started back to the parking lot.

The sleek dark blue car he had bought Brandy pulled out of the lot and headed down the driveway that wove past the kennel. Evidently, she had decided to pick him up. Holding Pepe close, Eric ran across the yard toward the road.

Somehow, they would all be okay. They would get back to Austin and the army would have things under control and maybe Rachel really was alive and Paul was just strung out on drugs and...

The car roared past him. Brandy didn't even turn her head to look at him. Eric frantically waved after her, but the car kept going. The wheels kicked up a thick plume of dust that engulfed him as he staggered to a halt. He stood in the middle of the lane in shock. Instinctively, he fumbled in his pocket for his phone so he could call her and beg her to turn around. It wasn't there. Instead, there was the tiny velvet box that held the diamond engagement ring.

Pepe licked Eric's cheek and snuggled under his chin.

It wasn't even eight o'clock in the morning yet and his world was over.

And far beyond the tiny bed and breakfast, the world was entering its final death throes.

Eric sat on the front porch of the B & B in numb silence. Pepe sniffed around the steps, but stayed close. Eric couldn't even fully comprehend that Brandy had truly left him behind. He kept expecting the car to return once she calmed down, but the lane remained empty.

5.
Death on the Doorstop

After an hour, Eric slowly stood and called Pepe to him. Though he hated to admit it, Brandy was not returning any time soon. Maybe once her anger cooled down she would return.

As he opened the door to enter the bed and breakfast, he noted the distinct lack of cooking smells. Usually Mrs. Waskom was in the kitchen cooking a delicious breakfast that was set out on the table around eight-thirty. He took a step inside, the wood floor creaking under him. The sound seemed to fill the building. He had the uneasy feeling he was all alone. Since they had arrived a few days ago, Brandy and Eric had been the only guests, but Mrs. Waskom was always about by this time. Curious, he strode through the foyer and hallway filled with antiques toward the back of the house where the refurbished kitchen was located.

He found it empty.

Feeling anxious, Eric walked back down the hall and checked in the parlor and the small office tucked off it. No one was in sight. The world felt frighteningly empty. Ill at ease, he walked over to the fireplace and snagged a poker from an ornate stand next to it. Gazing down at the handle clutched in his hand, he saw that he was trembling. To settle his nerves he took several deep breaths. The uneasiness he had felt the day before was swelling into an overwhelming fear and he struggled to gain control of it.

The front door of the house suddenly slammed open. He let out a yelp, started, and almost fell backwards over a chair. Pepe began to bark furiously.

Mrs. Waskom appeared in the doorway to the parlor looking flushed and agitated.

"You need to leave," she said bluntly. "Now. I'm leaving with my kids to join my husband at Fort Hood and I'm closing the bed and breakfast."

"My girlfriend left without me," Eric said awkwardly.

Mrs. Waskom blinked in surprise. "Damn. You had a fight?"

"Something like that." Eric picked up Pepe, but held onto the poker. "Why are you leaving?"

"My husband called and told me its getting worse. It's spreading, whatever *it* is. People going crazy and attacking each other." She hesitated. "He said I needed to get to Fort Hood before this thing explodes. He says they can't get it under control."

Eric's throat felt painfully dry and he swallowed hard. "I noticed on the TV that the higher population areas are having a lot more trouble. You might be safer here."

She laughed with amusement. "Sorry, but I'd rather take my chances with a fort full of armed soldiers than stay out in the middle of nowhere."

Eric shifted Pepe's warm little body in his arms. "I don't have anywhere to go. I have three hundred dollars in cash and my credit cards. If you let me stay here, I can watch over the bed and breakfast and the barn until you get back."

Mrs. Waskom fidgeted for a second before saying, "Look, you could come with us."

Eric felt sorely tempted, but the memory of the televised map highlighting all the hotspots of the violent outbreak sprung to the forefront of his mind. "I'd rather stay here. You can charge me for my stay."

"I have Felipe putting the horses out in the pasture along with bales of hay and sacks of feed. They'll be fine until I get back. But..." She pondered the offer again. "I guess you can stay. Seeing as you don't have a car and the bus that comes through town isn't coming today..."

Eric sighed with relief. "Thank you."

"Let me show you where everything is," Mrs. Waskom said, holding out her hand.

He was confused for a second then realized what she was waiting for. He quickly took out all his cash from his wallet and handed her two of his credit cards. Her fingers snapped around the money and she shoved the wad into her pocket.

"I'll make this fast," she said.

In ten minutes, he understood where all the food was, the emergency generator, the fuse box, the propane tanks, and the shotgun.

"I don't think you'll need it, but just in case," she said, patting the weapon.

Pepe curled up against his chest during the tour, looking pensive and a little sleepy. Eric felt much the same way. He had hardly slept the night before and the emotional drama of the morning had him utterly drained of energy.

When Mrs. Waskom finally ran out to her car packed with kids, Eric shut the door behind her with a finality that unnerved him. He listened to the car roar away, resisting the urge to run out and wave it down. Intellectually he knew he was doing the right thing even if his nerves didn't.

The world returned to a state of eerie silence.

Slowly, he trudged back up the stairs to the bedroom and flipped on the TV. Holding Pepe tightly, he flopped down on the bed.

"...*San Antonio authorities report increasing violence and residents are advised to stay home, barricade their doors and windows, and stay put. Emergency Rescue Centers are being set up, but as the infected escalate in numbers, it is becoming increasingly difficult to determine which areas are actually safe within San Antonio and other Texas cities.*"

Eric watched with morbid fascination as the footage of bloodied, crazed people rampaging through various cities flashed on the screen. A warning label in the corner of the screen announcing scenes of a "disturbing nature" amused him. The whole world was a scene of a "disturbing nature." Videos of mutilated, insane people invading Red Square in the shadow of the Kremlin clearly revealed that the violence was not isolated to just the United States. If the violence was the result of actions by terrorists, they had set off attacks all over the world.

As the news reports droned on, Eric felt his numbed mind trying to cope with Brandy leaving and the horrors that now filled the outside world. Pepe fell asleep next to him and snored loudly. At some point, he also fell asleep.

Eric woke to Pepe barking hysterically near the end of the bed toward the door to the hall. By the shadows filling in the room, Eric ascertained it was late in the afternoon. The television was still on and the map of the United States was now riddled with nasty little red dots

Pepe bounced on all four legs, barking as loudly as he could. Gripping the poker tightly in his hand, Eric slid off the bed and stumbled toward the bedroom door. His right leg was still asleep and he rubbed it to get the blood running.

Then he heard the loud thump down below.

"Brandy?" His voice cracked. He swallowed hard, and tried again. "Brandy, is that you?"

Pepe growled low in his throat as Eric slowly opened the bedroom door.

Again there was a loud bang down below.

Eric crept out into the hallway. Pepe didn't care about caution and tore down the stairs, barking.

"Pepe!"

Eric gave up and barged down the stairs. His little dog stood growling, two feet away from the front door. Eric's gaze was drawn to the stained glass window set in the heavy oak door. Dimly, he could make out the form of a person.

"Hello?" His voice cracked again. He attempted to muster up some saliva to coat his throat so he could speak clearly. "Who is there?"

A very low moan was his answer. The form on the other side of stained glass slammed into the door again.

Pepe's barking and growling became even more crazed. Warily, Eric backed up the stairs toward a window up near the landing.

"Pepe, calm down," he whispered, but the dog didn't care to obey. Carefully, Eric slid the curtain back. He could clearly see the sprawl of the porch and the figure standing outside the front door.

"Shit," he muttered.

A solider or what remained of a solider was standing outside the door. How the soldier could be up and walking around was beyond Eric's understanding. He was stripped down to just his pants and boots with his shirt hanging in long strips around his bloodied torso. Both the soldier's arms were missing as well as a good portion of the right side of his face. Eric slumped to the stairs and took several deep breaths.

"This can't be happening."

Pepe darted up the stairs, hopped onto Eric's lap, then launched himself up onto the windowsill to let the man on the porch know just how much he did not approve of his presence. The mutilated face of the solider swung about. He apparently saw the little dog for he staggered determinedly toward the window.

"Crap," Eric exclaimed, grabbed his dog, and bolted down the stairs.

To his horror, the soldier began to bang his head hard against the window.

"Okay, this is wrong. He shouldn't be able to do that or even walk around," Eric said aloud. "Hell, should I call 911? Or go outside and help him...?"

Pepe twisted around in Eric's grasp trying to see the window, growling viciously.

The humane thing to do, Eric thought, was to go outside and try to calm down the solider and treat his wounds. But if the soldier was infected with whatever was making people violent, maybe he was contagious. Considering the solider was banging his head as hard as he could against the base of the window, Eric was guessing he was infected.

"Need to check the TV," he decided and started back up the stairs.

As Eric passed the window, he heard the solider hissing and growling. He carefully pulled open the curtain an inch to see the man still banging his forehead against the base of the window. It was set high, so without arms, it was all the solider could really do to try to break in. The terribly wounded man saw Eric and began to howl. His twisted mouth opened and a gush of blood frothed over his lips and chin.

Eric let the curtain fall back and staggered back up the stairs. Clutching Pepe, he ran back to his room.

6.
Battling Death

None of this makes sense, Eric thought as he watched the TV.

The news continuously broadcast scenes of burning cities, horribly disfigured people tearing through city streets, disturbing footage of the "infected" apparently eating other people, and clips from a CDC press conference where a very pale woman said, "the dead are returning to life and attacking the living."

Pepe had abandoned him to growl and claw at the bottom of the bedroom door. The banging continued downstairs.

Eric flipped the channel and an Asian scientist was in mid-sentence. "...*unknown contagion is reanimating the corpses of those attacked by the infected.*"

Another man seated next to the scientist scoffed at this. "*That is ludicrous. It is obvious that this is a biological attack of terrifying proportions and whatever agent is being used is provoking people to acts of insanity.*"

"*Have you seen the footage?*" the scientist answered angrily. "*Have you seen them eating other people? Have you seen the infected with missing limbs, organs falling out of their bodies, walking down the streets? Have you? Because how can you not see that obviously-*"

The sound of glass shattering caused Eric to jump up. He immediately turned off the TV, breathing heavily as he listened to the sounds below. Tossing the remote onto the bed, he grabbed up the poker he had carried upstairs earlier. Pepe's tiny body was bouncing all around as he prepared to do battle.

"Okay, so, basically, that guy is dead and wants to eat us," Eric informed Pepe.

The dog threw him a dark look as if to say *d'oh* and continued barking.

With a shaking hand, Eric reached toward the doorknob. The pounding continued downstairs and he hesitated. The shotgun Mrs. Waskom had for protection was on the top shelf of the pantry in the kitchen. If he had been thinking straight and not about Brandy leaving him, he would have brought it up with him. Now he had to go down the stairs to get the gun before anymore of the living dead arrived.

"Zombies," he muttered "who would have thought it?"

He pulled the door open and Pepe immediately rushed downstairs again.

"Dammit, Pepe," Eric exclaimed, and hurried after the dog. Pepe was fearless and that fact terrified him. If anything happened to his little companion, it would devastate him. Eric would have to keep a leash on him at all times.

Pepe stopped on the step above the window and barked at the dead solider still systematically banging its head against the broken window. The pane had shattered in the corner where the solider continued to slam its head. Only a few large pieces had fallen out of the frame leaving most of the window still intact.

As the pale dead eye of the solider fastened on Eric, it began an ungodly howl.

"Crap!" Eric scooted down the stairs, hugging the wall in an attempt to keep far away from the bloodied creature. Realistically, he had nothing to fear since it had no arms, but he didn't want to take any risks.

He ran down the hallway of the slowly darkening farmhouse, feeling lightheaded and a little sick. He hadn't eaten all day and his brain was foggy and his body sluggish. As soon as he dealt with the creature outside, he would need to eat something and get his wits about him.

The kitchen was dark and foreboding when he entered. The warmth and beauty of the room was now lost in the late afternoon shadows filling it. He glanced toward the back door and was relieved to see it was shut with the locks engaged. Lifting the poker in one hand he slowly approached the closed door of the large pantry. Was there a window to the outside inside? He hadn't noticed before. What if something was in there waiting for him?

Pepe skittered into the kitchen, rushed up to the pantry, and waited for him expectantly.

"Anyone in there, boy?" he asked the dog.

The dog yawned in response.

"Okay, I'm trusting you on this."

Eric took a deep breath and pulled the pantry door open. Darkness filled the interior and the dim light from the kitchen barely made a dent in the gloom. With a trembling hand, he fumbled for the light switch and quickly flipped it on. Light flooded the pantry revealing the nicely stocked shelves filling its windowless interior. With a little bark, Pepe darted in and began to chew at the bottom of a bag of dog food resting under a shelf.

"In a moment, Pepe. Need to take care of the dead guy first."

Reaching up, he fumbled for the shotgun. It felt odd in his hands as he pulled it off the shelf.

"I can do this."

He took a deep breath. Breaking open the action of the shotgun, he checked the breach of the barrels to make sure the weapon was loaded. To his relief, it was. Snapping the action back into place, he took another shivering breath and tried to steady his nerves. A trickle of sweat slid down the bridge of his nose. He brushed it away and quickly adjusted his glasses.

"Okay, Pepe, you stay here and eat. I'll go kill the zombie."

Eric stepped out of the pantry and meant to lock Pepe in it, but the little dog went skittering past him and bolted into the hall. Within seconds he heard Pepe again barking at the zombie. He quickly followed, holding the shotgun tightly in his moist hands.

"You can do this," he chanted, trying to convince himself. "You can do this."

Eric's thumb played lightly with the safety catch as he moved toward the front door. He could see Pepe on the stairs angrily barking at the zombie. Eric's plan was simple. He would step out, shoot the zombie, then head back inside to start boarding up the windows. It was so easy it had to work.

The steady pounding of the zombie's forehead against the window reassured him it hadn't moved. As a precaution, Eric looked out another window and scanned the front yard and porch. There was no sign of any other undead creatures.

"Okay, Pepe, you keep him distracted and I'm going to shoot him," Eric said to the dog.

Unlocking the door, he gulped and tried to steady his nerves. The sound of the zombie banging against the window ended abruptly. Pepe immediately scampered down the stairs.

"Shit!"

Eric wrenched the door open and stepped outside in one swift motion.

The zombie staggered toward him. An eerie howl rose from its throat and its tongue lolled in its open mouth.

Pepe hustled his little body over to the zombie. The dog grabbed the shoelaces of the creature's combat boot and began to try to wrestle it. Meanwhile, Eric fought the instinct to run away. With trembling hands, he raised the shotgun and fired. The recoil sent him stumbling backward a few feet.

The buckshot hit the zombie's bare chest and it jerked from the impact. Recovering, it continued toward Eric. Eric was stunned by the zombie's quick recovery and he stared down at the shotgun not understanding how he had failed. Pepe's growls alerted Eric and he looked up. The zombie was closing in. Eric raised the shotgun again, prepared himself for the recoil, and fired.

This time the buckshot ripped through the thing's neck and the lower half of its face. The zombie kept coming.

"Oh, God," Eric prayed.

He tried to fire again.

The shotgun clicked empty.

He hadn't brought any more shells with him.

"Oh, crap," he exclaimed.

Pepe suddenly cried out in pain and Eric's gaze dropped swiftly to the little guy. The zombie's foot had caught one of Pepe's paws and the little dog darted back, favoring his front leg.

The zombie walked straight into the end of the shotgun and snapped its bloodied teeth at Eric. Acting on instinct, Eric shoved it hard into the creature's mouth and pushed the creature away from him. The zombie staggered back, struggling to keep its balance, but it had no arms to steady itself. It toppled over onto the porch.

"Pepe, back!" Eric ordered and to his surprise the little dog stopped in mid-attack on the zombie's shoelaces.

Grabbing up a heavy iron chair, Eric approached the wildly thrashing zombie. Eric grimaced and tried hard not to look at its battered flesh as he brought the chair leg down on the creature's head. There was a sickening sucking sound as the metal leg sank through one eye socket and into the zombie's head. Pressing downward, Eric felt bone and brain matter give way as the metal leg sank into the thing's skull. The body spasmed a few times then was still.

Eric reeled away from the dead solider, gasping for air, and collapsed onto the porch. Pepe sauntered over to Eric, seeming quite satisfied with the whole situation. He wiggled onto Eric's lap and gave him a few licks with his pink tongue. His owner, overwhelmed at what had just happened, kept staring at the zombie's still form.

"It's really happening," he said finally.

Pepe looked at Eric with an exasperated air then skipped off back into the house to make a run at the pantry and the dog food.

Eric sluggishly climbed to his feet as he studied his surroundings. There was no one else in sight and the clouds overhead looked ominous. He had maybe two hours of light before sunset. He needed to do some serious planning.

Eric's gaze thoughtfully swept over the farmhouse and he realized he had completely overlooked the old fashioned storm shutters locked in place next to all the windows.

Excited at the discovery, he quickly moved to slam the shutters closed over the broken window and slid the securing bar into place.

"Freaking perfect!"

Deciding to hurry while he had no unwanted visitors, he closed the front door to keep Pepe inside. Running around the bottom floor of the house, Eric closed all the shutters and locked them. He wasn't too sure if zombies would figure out how to open the shutters, but he was hoping they wouldn't. His heart thumped so hard in his chest it hurt, but it felt good to be actually doing something productive.

Once the windows were all secured, he slipped back into the house and bolted the door. The power was still on, which he hoped was a good sign, and he flipped lights on as he walked to the kitchen. With all the windows shuttered, the house was very dark. The gloom was a little frightening, but he knew the house was secure.

Eric exhaled with relief as he entered the kitchen. Pepe was still in the pantry eating out of the torn dog food bag. When Eric snagged a box of shotgun shells off the top shelf, Pepe barely acknowledged him and kept eating.

After loading the gun, Eric laid it on the counter and took several deep breaths. He was dizzy. He needed to eat. He found a loaf of multi-grain bread in the breadbox; old fashioned peanut butter swimming in oil in the pantry, and homemade strawberry preserves in the fridge. He couldn't make his sandwiches fast enough and he ate them with desperate bites. He put a bowl of water down for Pepe and gulped milk directly from the jug.

When the phone rang, he jumped and almost choked on his sandwich. Chewing quickly, he swallowed before grabbing the phone off the hook.

"Hello?"

"Who's this?" a gruff voice said. "Where is Mrs. Waskom?"

"Fort Hood. She went to be with her husband. I'm one of the guests. Who's this?"

"Sheriff Davis. I am trying to account for all the people not here at the shelter."

"The shelter?" Eric swallowed down more milk to clear his throat.

"Yes, the shelter. We're at the community center. You should get down here as soon as possible. We got a doctor here to treat the wounded and we're armed and ready to stand until the army gets here."

"Wounded?"

"Yes, wounded. Army helicopter went down outside of town. Some of the soldiers were in a bad shape when the rescuers went out to get them. Some of our folks got hurt and some of the soldiers are not doing so hot."

Eric's eyes widened a little. That explained the solider on the porch. He had a pretty good idea why the helicopter went down.

"Look, sir, I don't know if you have been watching the news-"

"I'm following the orders that FEMA handed down for our area. Gather everyone into one spot, treat the wounded, and wait for the National Guard or Army to come for us. Now, son, I suggest you get down here."

"You can't keep the wounded in there, sir. The news says the wounded will end up just like those things attacking everyone. End up a zombie." Eric gripped the edge of the sink tightly. He couldn't believe that the infection of the undead had already reached this far out into the countryside.

"Look, son, I don't look kindly at zombie talk. I suggest you get down here immediately. I can send a squad car for you." The voice on the other end was resolute.

"I...would rather stay here," Eric answered, and began counting out the shells in the box he had found.

"I'm not coming to get you when the rescue team gets here," the Sheriff said darkly.

Eric ran his fingers through his hair as he realized how little ammunition he truly had. "I...think I'd rather take my chances here, sir. If you've got wounded in your rescue station, it is going to get bad really fast."

There was a long, agitated silence on the other end of the phone, then the Sheriff said, "Suit yourself," and hung up.

Eric hung up the phone, then on impulse picked it back up and dialed Brandy's number.

"We're sorry. All circuits are busy," a voice said.

Eric should have known the cell phone companies were overloaded. He set the phone down again and pushed his glasses back up the bridge of his nose.

Pepe sat next to his feet and stared at him pensively.

"Oh, shit," was all Eric could think to say. "Oh, shit."

7.
The Day Worsens

Eric took another gulp of milk, then patted Pepe. The dog responded with an enormous burp and Eric couldn't help but laugh.

"Went a little crazy there, did you?" he said to the little dog.

Pepe wagged his tail with satisfaction.

The house was dreary with all the windows shuttered. It made him uneasy. There was at least two more hours of sunlight left in the day and if the town was about to turn into zombie central, he needed to make plans.

Eric took the time to put all the food items away, then picked up the shotgun. Reloading it was his first priority. Once he had it loaded and ready for the next encounter with the zombies, he shoved the rest of the shells in his pocket.

"Okay, Pepe, this is the plan. We're going to go make sure there are no zombies around, then we're going outside-"

Pepe thumped his tail hard at the word *outside* and Eric realized how long it had been since the little dog had been able to do his business.

"Okay, definitely that is a major priority. We're going to come up with an escape plan and figure out what we are doing next."

Pepe strutted out of the kitchen, and Eric followed.

The second floor was awash with dim sunlight. The overcast skies made it a little darker than usual, but it felt better than the gloomy downstairs. He wasn't sure he was glad they had been the only guests or not. Being on his own meant he had the final say in anything he planned, but it felt lonely being the only one in the house. Well, alone except for Pepe.

In the room he had shared with Brandy, he pulled out his suitcase and tried to ignore the heartache he felt when her sweet scent wafted up from the bed. She always slathered herself in body lotion before bed and the sheets still smelled like jasmine. Digging through his suitcase, he found the small binoculars he had brought for bird watching. Brandy had given him hell for bringing them and called him a nerd, but he felt smug now that his little hobby gave him a tool to protect himself. He picked up the small book he had brought with photos of all the indigenous birds in the region.

"Think they have one for zombies?" Eric wondered aloud. "You know, one that has photos of all the terrible versions of them."

Pepe tilted his head as if pondering the question.

"Maybe we should make that book. Starting with the armless army guy." Eric let out a small, nervous laugh.

He tossed the book into the suitcase and pulled out Pepe's leash. The little dog did a flying leap onto the bed and scrambled onto the suitcase with his tail wagging anxiously. Eric felt bad for making Pepe wait so long to relieve himself and quickly hooked the leash onto the small dog's collar. The second it was on, the dog jumped to the floor and headed out the door.

Slinging the binoculars around his neck and grabbing the shotgun, Eric hurried to keep up with the dog. Pepe started down the stairs, but Eric stopped him.

"Check for zombies first, Pepe."

The dog gave him a nasty look, but followed.

Eric hurried to the doors that led onto the upstairs porch. White wicker chairs and a table were arranged outside so guests could star gaze or just relax on a nice afternoon. Stepping out, Eric looked over the rail. Nothing lurked below. Raising his binoculars, he began to survey the surrounding area as best he could from his vantage point.

The horses in the pasture were the only signs of life other than the sparrows overhead. Eric leaned over the railing as far as he dared to look toward the tops of the buildings in the far distance. He couldn't see the town clearly from this point.

"Okay, we'll check the other side, then go down," he told Pepe.

Eric was sure from the dog's expression that if he could have done the one legged dance, he would. He dragged the poor dog through the hallway that curved around the stairwell and opened to a bank of tall windows. Looking out, he could see into the gardens, the parking lot, and off to the second barn used for farm vehicles. Again, nothing sinister was in sight.

Raising his binoculars, he attempted to view the town. The trees were lush and green as spring took hold of the world and the leafy boughs blocked his view. By moving from window to window, he finally he managed to see a sliver of one of the streets. It was empty.

"Okay, let's go down and check it out."

Pepe immediately pulled at the leash and tried to scoot down the stairs. He wasn't barking, which was reassuring, but Eric didn't know if he could trust him since the dog was so desperate to relieve himself. Since the windows were secured, he had to resort to studying the front porch through the peephole. Pepe insistently scratched at the bottom of the door until Eric unlocked it and swung it open.

A large cloud of flies hovered over the dead body of the solider, but nothing else was moving except the swaying treetops. Relieved, Eric hurried after Pepe who was straining at the end of the leash to reach the yard. The second the dog hit the grass, he let out a powerful stream of urine and managed to poop all at the same time.

"That's really impressive, Pepe."

Eric was rewarded with a look that distinctively said *fuck you*.

When Pepe was done, they warily strolled across the gravel parking lot toward the big barn that housed the tractor, mowers and other vehicles used on the property. Eric popped the safety off on the shotgun and looped Pepe's leash around his wrist. Fear was eating away at his stomach.

Eric really didn't have any sort of plan, but he knew that if the town went zombie, staying in the B & B was not the best idea. The storm shutters would only hold out for so long. He wanted a clear plan on how to retreat and escape if the farmhouse ended up under siege. Where he would go, he had no idea, but getting away from the infected area seemed like a good idea. He was hoping that maybe he could find a location further out in the country that was more secure. But then again, it was tempting to just hole up and try to ride it out.

Just as he reached the barn he stopped in his tracks, regarding the barn.

Pepe moved to the end of his leash and glanced back at him expectantly. If the dog wasn't going nuts, that had to mean it was safe, yet he couldn't help but stare at the slightly open door with a little trepidation. Finally, he managed to settle his nerves with a few deep breaths and opened it up.

The barn was empty except for the farm vehicles carefully parked in their proper places. There was a mower, a small tractor, and several small box trailers and dump beds against one wall.

But what made his heart beat faster was a four wheel ATV sitting nearby. It was grimy and well-used, but it could easily spirit him and Pepe away.

Rushing over to it, he began to study it intently, trying to remember how to drive the damn thing. He was pretty sure he could figure it out. His hand slid over the handlebars and he grinned down at Pepe.

"These things go fast, boy. This will work for us."

Pepe responded by marking the tire with a nice little stream.

"I guess it's ours now," Eric said with a laugh.

He pushed his glasses up on his nose as he pondered his options. There was a box trailer attached to the back of the ATV. It, too, had sturdy wheels and a wide tread. He could easily load it up with supplies and tie them down.

"Okay, this looks good. Real good. It's not a car, but it can maybe get us to one."

The next hour was a rush of activity. To his surprise, he found the owner's manual in the desk in Mrs. Waskom's office and gave it quick read through. He gassed up the vehicle at the gas pump next to the barn then drove it over to the back porch of the house with Pepe perched on his lap. When he had first been shown around the house, Mrs. Waskom had demonstrated how to use the inflatable slide that would whisk them down to safety in case of fire. He made sure to get the ATV set up so if he did make a quick exit from the house, he would slide right down to the ATV. Then he loaded up the box trailer with canned goods, water jugs, and food for Pepe. Tying up a pillow and comforter as a bedroll, he also added that to the load.

Eric was just finishing knotting the last of the rope used to secure the load when Pepe went into a barking fit. His heart began to pump fiercely in his chest as he was seized with the cold hand of terror. Fighting it off, he slowly edged his way along the back of the house until he could peer around the corner. To his amazement, he saw Brandy walking up the long winding road toward the B & B. Her hair was blown across her face by the gusts of the wind from the approaching storm and she was clutching her cell phone tight in one hand.

"Brandy!" He gasped with delight, unable to fully grasp that she had returned.

Pepe continued to bark angrily. He couldn't blame the little dog. Brandy had been a total bitch that morning.

"Brandy, baby! Oh, my gawd! Where is the car?" He started toward her, dragging Pepe behind him. The little dog at first resisted then changed his mind and began to dart in front of Eric's legs, almost tripping him.

"Brandy!" Eric waved at her, grinning, his heart bursting with happiness.

Slowly, she raised her head. From the distance he could see that one cheek was gone and there was a deep gash in her forehead. Her exposed perfect white teeth snapped as her murky eyes fastened hungrily on him.

Then with an ungodly shriek, she charged toward him.

8.
Fighting Back the Dead

Despite her torn face, blank eyes, and terrifying shriek, Eric couldn't accept that Brandy had joined the ranks of the undead. Staring blankly at her approaching form, he stood with the shotgun dangling in his hand. It was difficult for his brain to equate her torn visage with the one he loved so much. Her beautiful legs were splattered with blood and one of them was twisted making her movement toward him jerky and inhuman.

Yet, it was Brandy: her gorgeous streaked hair, her swaying breasts, her immaculately manicured hands reaching for him. Her dead eyes and ruined cheek destroyed the illusion that she was alive and returning to be with him and Pepe.

Pepe was in a barking fit at his feet. The little dog's warning finally registered and his senses returned to normal. Eric's survival instinct finally kicked in and he raised the shotgun.

It was obviously difficult for the undead Brandy to make it up the incline of the hill, but she was doing her best to reach him. Her leg kept twisting, turning her body to one side with each step. She had to swing her other leg around to redirect herself toward Eric and the little dog. Her gait was ponderous and it ripped at Eric's heart to see her in this condition.

Pepe strained at the end of his leash, putting himself directly between Eric and the zombie. His shrill barks of anger grew fiercer as she approached.

"Pull the trigger," Eric whispered to himself, but his finger seemed to have trouble responding. He became aware of the tears rushing down his cheeks as he sniffled loudly. "Pull the trigger."

Another voice, maybe the voice of reason, whispered in his thoughts to flip off the safety and his thumb did so. The same voice urged him to raise the gun higher and he did. But still, his finger on the trigger would not obey his order to pull it.

"Brandy," he wailed in a soft voice.

This couldn't be real. She couldn't be a zombie. She was just hurt. Maybe she had been in a car accident. She was coming for help. There was just no way she could be one of the undead.

Brandy kicked Pepe aside just like she always tended to do and the little dog yelped. Her lovely hands tipped in long pink nails reached out to grip Eric's shoulders and he felt them slide along the material of his shirt. The gun was lodged firmly between their bodies, holding them apart. The terrible wound on her cheek revealed her lolling tongue and champing teeth and he gasped as she tried to pull him close.

With a whimper of despair, Eric shoved her away with the gun and she stumbled back on her broken leg. Howling with frustration, Brandy launched her wounded body at him. This time he raised the gun a little higher and shoved the barrel into her open mouth. She didn't seem to notice as she her perfectly shaped white teeth ground against the metal.

Pepe hysterically barked at their feet, pulling on Brandy's shoe to get her away from Eric.

"Brandy," Eric said, squeezing his eyes shut. "I'm really sorry."

At last, his finger obeyed his inner voice. The bark of the shotgun firing filled the air and echoed around the farmhouse. Eric was able to handle the recoil a bit better this time and stood his ground as he fired again. He could not stand to see Brandy's torn face or witness her final death.

Pepe lapsed into silence and Brandy's growls ceased as the echo of the second gunshot faded away. Eric felt the shotgun grow heavy with the weight of her body. He lowered the barrel and felt her slip off. Her body crumpled before him with a heavy thud.

With tears blurring his vision, he dared to glance down at her fallen corpse. Her face was turned away from him with her hair covering her features like a death shroud.

Pepe sat next to the body and whined sadly in his throat. The sound unleashed Eric's agony and he fell to his knees sobbing. Pepe laid a little paw on Brandy's arm and began to piteously howl. Together, the man and his dog mourned a woman that had been a part of their life for the last two years and despite everything she had done, they both had loved in their own way.

Time passed as they sat together mourning. At some point, Brandy had turned back and returned to the town. Obviously, something had happened on the road.

Finally, Eric took off his glasses and wiped his eyes. "She was coming back," Eric said to Pepe. "I bet she was sorry and was coming back to us."

Pepe looked over his shoulder at Eric and whined a little.

Eric would have forgiven her and together they would have faced the undead horde. It was easy to imagine their reunion, their stand against the zombies, their fight to freedom and safety with little Pepe at their side.

It was too easy to imagine and too painful to realize it never would happen.

Instead, Brandy had died somewhere nearby and he had given her final, terrible death.

Somewhere nearby...

He scrambling to his feet, he shoved his glasses back on. Pepe looked up in alarm.

"There are more out there."

Pepe hopped up to all fours, alert.

Eric quickly broke open the shotgun and began to reload it with the shells from his pocket. He was suddenly and terrifyingly aware of how exposed he was.

Snapping the action back into place, he began to walk carefully toward the front of the house. He knew the front door was shut and therefore nothing could have slipped inside. The shadows were growing longer and something could easily be lurking in the bushes or behind the trees.

In actuality, it was standing in the parking lot looking one way then the other. Maybe it had heard him and Pepe and wasn't sure where the sound had come from. Voices either echoed around the house or were carried off by the wind coming up the back of the hill from the pasture.

The very tall zombie had ebony skin, a shaved head and was wearing army fatigues. The dead man's face and chest were smeared in blood and chunks of flesh and Eric felt his stomach lurch. It was probably Brandy's blood. Before he could even formulate a plan, Pepe charged forward on his leash and began to bark at the dead thing.

The pale eyes of the creature scanned the area and found Eric. With an unholy scream, it charged toward him.

"Dammit, Pepe!"

Eric ran toward the front door. The dog ran next to him, still barking. To his horror, Eric realized halfway to the porch he was not going to make it to safety. Swinging the gun around, he aimed at the creature's head and fired. The zombie was so close, the buckshot flayed its face opened and destroyed its eyes. It screeched in frustration as it was instantly blinded, but continued forward. Eric realized that the buckshot was only going to be effective at close range.

"Shit!"

The zombie was still floundering in his direction and the porch was still not close enough to reach without risking the zombie's clutches. Looking around in desperation, he spotted a shovel set aside with other gardening tools. The tools had probably been abandoned this morning when everything had gone to hell.

"Pepe, shut up!"

He was rewarded with a stunned look and silence.

Not wanting to waste the ammunition and feeling a deep terrible anger at the murderous thing for what it had done to Brandy, Eric picked up the shovel. Letting go of Pepe's leash, he motioned for the dog to sit. Pepe obeyed.

Slowly, Eric began to circumvent the blind zombie, trying to get behind it. The dead man floundered through the garden, banging into trees and foliage, as it continued toward the spot that it had last seen Eric. Pepe sat uneasily, watching his master with bright eyes with his gaze flicking toward the zombie warily. Eric pointed at Pepe to stay once more and took his time to move quietly around some benches. The zombie banged into the side of the benches and staggered a few feet to one side. Correcting itself, it stumbled again toward where Pepe waited.

Eric set one foot on a bench and heaved himself up praying it wouldn't creak. It didn't. Then he stood, legs apart, and lifted the shovel over his head.

"Hey, fuckhead," he shouted.

The zombie whipped around and started toward him.

Eric screamed in anger and slammed the side edge of the shovel down onto the zombie's head. There was a sickening sound, like a cantaloupe being dropped on the floor, as the shovel smashed into the creature's head, splitting apart the skin and bone. The zombie stopped in its tracks and wobbled on its feet. Eric managed to draw the shovel back and slam it down again. This time it sank deep into the zombie's head and the creature fell to the ground, truly dead.

Eric felt sick to his stomach, but jumped down off the bench and drove the shovel into the back of the man's head a few more times. He could see now that the solider had been attacked from behind. Large chunks of flesh were torn from his shoulder and back.

"Pepe, come here," Eric ordered as his nerves steadied.

The little dog, which seemed properly impressed by his master's prowess, trotted over trailing his leash.

Eric pulled the shovel free of the zombie's head and wiped the brains and blood off on the grass. To his surprise, he saw the man had a revolver still tucked into his holster. With trembling fingers, he retrieved it, then backed away from the body.

"Okay, we're going into the house," Eric said in a quivering voice.

Pepe waited for him to grab the end of the leash then together they hurried back to the house. Eric took one last long look around the property before slamming the door shut behind him, sealing him and Pepe into the safety of the old farmhouse.

9.
Revelations

That night was rough. He opened a bottle of wine and drank the whole thing while watching the news on the TV. He let Pepe up on the bed with him, something Brandy would never do, and managed to eat some roasted chicken he had found in the refrigerator and some left over pie. It was hard to do anything other than cry as the news continued to show the end of the world and Brandy's body lay prone beneath the bedroom window.

Today was the day he was supposed to slip the big diamond ring on her finger and instead he had killed her. Well, killed her a second time. Still, Brandy was gone. Her beauty, her laugh, her smile, her kisses, everything. And though she had given him a rough time, cheated on him and had one of the worst tempers he had ever encountered, he had loved her. Now she was gone.

He fell asleep around midnight and didn't wake up until morning. Pepe woke him up with a cold nose to his forehead and an insistent whine. Pepe needed to go do his business.

Eric's head throbbed with a wine hangover and he grunted as he sat up. "You do realize there are zombies outside, right? And me taking you outside might get my ass eaten."

Pepe gave him an annoyed look and jumped down to the floor.

"Gimme a sec," Eric muttered.

He staggered into the bathroom, relieved himself, and then splashed cold water on his face to fully wake himself up. Pepe waited impatiently for him in the doorway, looking pretty disgruntled that Eric's bladder was empty while his was still full.

Eric snatched up the revolver and binoculars and began his rounds by looking out all the windows to make sure nothing was lurching around in the early morning. Brandy's body and that of the solider lay where he had left them. Nothing else stirred except for the Waskom cat stalking a bird.

"Okay, let's do this," Eric said in a voice that sounded a little stuffy from all his crying the night before.

Making sure Pepe was secure on the leash, he hurried down the stairs and double-checked through the peephole before opening the door.

The morning was glorious. The sunlight streaming through the trees was hazy and full of tiny motes of pollen. Spring flowers in all their colorful raiment flowed down the sides of the driveway and filled the garden. Birds sang in the trees and in the distance a rooster announced the morning routine. It was a perfect day. Well, except for the dead soldiers on the porch and in the garden and Brandy's body around the side of the house.

Pepe skipped down the steps and began sniffing around for the perfect place to relieve himself.

"I like it better when you dump and go," Eric chided him. "You know, zombies."

Pepe gave him a dark look and continued to nose around a birdbath.

Eric's gaze roamed toward driveway and he wondered where his car was located. Obviously, Brandy had almost made it back to the bed and breakfast. It was hard for him to believe she had walked miles and miles to get to the house. So far, the zombies didn't seem capable of deductive reasoning. He seriously doubted they even remembered their lives. So that meant the car was nearby.

Eric could feel his legs getting wobbly at the thought of taking such a big risk, but no more zombies had shown up last night. If things had gone down badly in the community center, they would be trapped inside the building.

Taking a deep breath, he rubbed the side of his nose nervously.

He could walk down the driveway and see if the car was somewhere along the side of the road. If it was intact, they could use that instead of the ATV to escape. It would be safer.

Maybe Brandy had seen the solider, not realized he was dead, stopped for help and...

That was always a possibility.

Right?

Pepe finished his business and kicked his back feet over the mess. It didn't do much to cover it, but Pepe seemed to think it helped. Skipping to the edge of his leash, the dog looked around then began to sniff at a statue.

If the dog seemed calm, then it should be okay. He was tempted to take the ATV, but he didn't want to disturb his carefully laid out exit plan. As long as Pepe was calm, he should be safe on foot.

Right?

Eric took a deep breath and looked down at the revolver in his hand. This was a better weapon. Faster. More destructive. He would aim for the head and it would be fast.

His stomach coiling into knots, he glanced over his shoulder at the closed door to the farmhouse.

Yeah.

The car would be good.

He started walking down the stone path to the parking lot. Pepe groused a little as he was pulled away from smelling all the fabulous scents hidden in the grass, but he followed. Eric's loafers crunched across the gravel parking lot as Pepe skipped along, his tiny feet expertly maneuvering over the rougher parts. Once they hit the paved road, Pepe began to dash about excitedly, sniffing every spot on the road just about. He didn't seem alarmed and didn't bark.

Eric walked briskly, the cool morning air soothing against his warm flesh. His nerves were on edge and he could feel his body temperature rising. Swallowing hard, he tried not to panic. The trees lining the road were full of singing birds and the branches swayed with the breeze in a soothing dance.

But he knew he could not relax, he could not drop his guard.

Pepe suddenly growled.

Eric spun around, the gun raised instantly.

A squirrel tittered angrily at Pepe then scampered up a tree.

Pepe barked after it with satisfaction, then looked at Eric's tense face as if to say *What?*

"No barking at squirrels, Pepe. Zombies only!" Eric lowered the gun and took a deep breath.

Pepe looked a bit disappointed with this order, turned, and kicked his back paws at Eric in disapproval.

The man and the dog continued their stroll, moving down the road and along the curve, losing sight of the house. Eric's heart began to thud harshly in his chest while his hands felt cold and clammy.

"A car is a good thing," he muttered, and kept walking.

He had to keep focused on the goal. The goal was safe passage.

They rounded another curve and the trees on the right-hand side of the road gave way to a long sloping view of a field full of bluebonnets, then to the town nestled at the bottom of the hill. Fumbling for his binoculars around his neck, he took a deep breath.

"Let's see what is going on, Pepe."

Main Street swam into view as he peered through the magnifying lenses. Eric scanned the view carefully, studying every doorway to the shops, the shadows, and the visible parking areas. He was relieved to see that the street was devoid of any life. He slid his gaze along the street to the old church that was a landmark in the town and the old city hall. If he remembered correctly, the community center was between them.

A squat building, the style of which was circa 1970, came into view and he adjusted the binoculars just a tad to zoom in on it. Long, glass windows were set into the pale orange bricks and enormous glass doors were set under a portico. This was obviously the front entrance. Objects appeared to be pushed up against the doors from inside. He moved the binoculars slowly down the side of the building. There was shadowy movement beyond the windows. The last window was not obscured by the trees or bushes bordering the building. He gasped and dropped his binoculars.

Blood. The window had been splashed with blood.

His hands trembling, Eric tried to steady his nerves. It was hard to breathe and he struggled to force air into his lungs. The undead citizens of the town were inside the community center.

Trapped.

That was a good thing. He had to remember that. It was a good thing they couldn't get out.

The wind rustled the wildflowers and tall grass before him. The world seemed serene and lovely this morning. Pepe busily scratched at the dirt next to the road and did not seem the least bit worried.

The road curved just ahead to meet the main street into town. Eric wasn't sure he wanted to go any further. He was about to turn back when a glint of glass in the trees caught his eye.

Taking a few steps forward, he raised his binoculars and adjusted the settings quickly. The dark blue car was nestled under the trees, the front hood bashed up against the shattered windshield. The driver's door was buckled, the door window smashed out and covered in blood. It was his car. It was the car Brandy had died in.

He lowered the binoculars and took a breath. His mind was whirling with the possibilities of what may have happened.

Brandy had realized she was wrong as she drove back to Austin and turned around. She was driving up to the bed and breakfast when the solider lunged out at the car. She swerved to avoid him, slammed into the tree, and broke her leg. The zombie reached through the broken window, grabbed her and...

Eric let out a strangled sob and took another breath.

Maybe that had happened.

Or...

Brandy had made it part of the way to Austin, suffered an attack, and wounded, tried to make it back to the bed and breakfast. But she died of her wounds before she made it up the hill and crashed into the tree.

Maybe.

Pulling off his glasses, he rubbed his nose.

Pepe began to eat some grass, and Eric pulled him back onto the road.

It didn't matter what had happened to Brandy. She was gone. Dead. Forever. And he and Pepe were alone in a town full of the dead. The only safe place for now was the house. Of course, how long that would be safe was a whole other story, but he didn't have the heart to move on just yet.

There was still work to be done before he and Brandy could be at peace and he also knew that he may not have much time to do it. Burying the dead was now a luxury. Brandy had always loved luxury.

She deserved it.

He would do it.

Fighting down his fear and feeling his determination giving him strength, he walked back up the hill to the farmhouse to bury his love.

10.
Despair

Despite himself, despite everything he had planned, despite all that he feared, despite the knowledge that the community center was full of the undead, Eric stayed in the B & B. At first it was because he was in no condition to travel, but after three days, it was because a deep malaise had sunk into his bones.

The night he put Brandy into her grave was the night he fell into bed drunk from three bottles of wine and slept through most of the next day. He woke up dizzy, sick and unsure of where he was for a moment.

Pepe, desperate to relieve himself, was good enough to do it in the bathroom next to the toilet and Eric felt a pang of remorse for letting the dog suffer. Yet he could hardly bring himself to crawl out of bed that day. All he wanted to do was lay in the bed, listening to the air conditioner hum, and watching TV.

The day after Brandy's death the networks continued with their live feed. From the expressions on the newscasters' faces and the continuing terrible news, it was obvious there was no going back. The world was ending and the dwindling TV audience, locked up in their homes and rescue centers, watched just like Eric did: in numb silence.

He tried calling his brother in Fort Worth, but the phone rang endlessly and never kicked over into voicemail. His parent's phone in Galveston had a busy signal. His sister's cheery voice exclaimed *hi* when he called her, but then immediately launched into urging him to leave a message.

Finally, needing food, he had ventured downstairs. The darkness was unnerving and he turned on all the lights. The brightness only added to his headache.

After a meal of leftovers, he sat down at the aging computer in Mrs. Waskom's office and tried to find any other news on the Internet. His email was a full of messages from friends, but they were now a day old. He answered every email and explained in detail his location. In his heart, he knew it was a fruitless endeavor, but he had to try. After an hour of responding to emails, he logged onto his IM service. None of his friends, co-workers or family members was logged on.

On his Facebook page he found a message from his sister saying that she was on her way with her kids to his parents' home to ride out the plague. He felt sick to his stomach when he read her message and was tormented by the thought of the busy signal he encountered whenever he called his folks. He tried not to think of what may have caused the phone to be off the hook.

That night, he opened another bottle of wine and drank straight from it while he tried all night to call his family.

No one ever answered.

By the next day, the major networks began to carry the feed from the emergency broadcast system. All the channels looped the same information endlessly and the news never seemed to be updated. He checked all the news websites again to find them unchanged. His emails remained unanswered. There were no new Facebook messages.

A random message came through on the chat just as he was about to log off.

It was from someone he didn't know and it read: *Are you really there?*

His hands trembling, he typed back that he was.

There was a long pause then more words spilled across the text box: *I'm afraid. They're outside the door.*

Eric let out a long sigh, then typed as he spoke aloud, "Are you alone?"

The words from a girl named Stephanie Brooks made him sigh sadly: *I'm alone. They're all dead. I'm scared. Can you come get me?*

Despite himself, Eric typed back, his voice a whisper, "Where are you?" Maybe he was giving her false hope, but if he could do something...

Pepe looked up at Eric with concern. He had been chewing happily on a stuffed toy, probably an antique.

"It's a girl, I think, somewhere else. Trapped by the zombies," Eric explained.

The dog continued to chew on the toy's foot, his eyes looking up at Eric thoughtfully.

Stephanie wrote: *St. Louis. Are you nearby? Can you get me? I can crawl out the window and jump down from the roof.*

Eric let out a long, strangled sigh of remorse. "I'm in Texas," he said softly as he typed. "I'm sorry, Stephanie."

It seemed painfully long before text wrote out: *It's okay. At least I'm not alone.*

For thirty minutes, they chatted back and forth. Stephanie explained she was home visiting from college when it had all gone to hell. He told her about Brandy and how Pepe was with him. She was worried about her cat that had run away when the zombies first stormed the house. She was in the attic, behind a thick oak door, on her laptop, hoping the Wi-Fi from the neighbors' house continued to hold up. Alone, scared and hungry, she was trying to find help when she had found him while searching for a family friend with Eric's name.

"She's so scared," Eric whispered to Pepe, "and I can't do anything."

The dog whined a little and started chewing on the toy's other foot.

He was typing out a message to her when suddenly the word *bye* appeared in the box.

Feeling sick to his stomach, he pressed ENTER to deliver his message and waited.

Despite her online status, she didn't answer.

He typed to her a few more times, but there was no response.

Her status remained online, but idle.

The next morning, groggy and hung over again, he checked online to see if she had ever answered. Gibberish filled the text screen. He logged off.

Overwhelmed, he fell to the floor and wept.

11.
Hope

Eric woke up with a cold nose pressed against his own. He groaned and ran a hand over his face feeling the scrubby nastiness of three days of no shaving scrape his palm. Opening his eyes, Pepe's worried expression came into view. He mumbled that he was okay and the little dog jumped down. The noon sun was pouring through the bedroom windows and the stained glass threw vibrant colors over the walls.

He had been dreaming about Stephanie and as the last threads of sleep faded from his brain, he let out a soft moan. Rolling off the bed onto the floor, he crawled to the bathroom and threw up. It was probably the best thing for his tired body considering how much he had drank the night before.

Pepe regarded him with a very serious expression on his little face through the whole process. When Eric half fell, half climbed into the shower with his clothes on and turned on the water full force, Pepe actually looked relieved.

Sitting under the slowly warming water, Eric sighed sorrowfully and thought of all that had happened the last few days with a startling amount of clarity, despite how much he had been drinking. The despair he had felt overwhelming him the last few days as Brandy's death, the probable deaths of his family, and the end of the world became a reality was still lingering, but was diminished by his growing determination.

Stephanie had just been a girl home from college. Ten years younger than he was, she had been on the cusp of her great college adventure and the beginning of her adult life. Instead of enjoying her spring break with her family, she had ended up barricaded in an attic trying to escape their hungry undead assault. It had hurt him to know he was her last friend in her life and he had not been able to help her. Her bravery, her determination, even to the end, to reach out and somehow find help, had touched him.

After he had accepted she was no longer at her computer or safe, and perhaps not even alive, he had drunk too much and had fallen asleep. He dreamed of her scrambling out the attic window and away from the zombies breaking in through the door. He had watched her through his murky dreamscape climb up onto the top of the roof and sit there, clutching a wind vane as the dead moaned all around her house. And just when she had given up all hope, a helicopter had zoomed down out of the sky and plucked her to safety. As dreams have a tendency to do, his had quickly shifted and he was sitting with Stephanie in the helicopter as Brandy turned in to the pilot's seat to say, "See, we're safe now."

He let out a soft moan and leaned his forehead against the wet tiles.

Pepe set his paws on the edge of the tub and stared up at him with concern.

"I'm okay," Eric assured him and stripped down to take a decent shower.

Now that his drunken binge was over and his head was clearing, he realized that he needed to decide right here and now if he wanted to live or not. The world was in its death throes, his family was most likely gone, Brandy was dead, and the last friend he may ever make was gone, too. All that was left was he and Pepe.

He looked over at the little dog anxiously watching him and felt a pang of guilt. How could he let himself go this far? Pepe needed him. The Jack Russell Terrier was faithful and loved him. Eric often called him "my furry little boy" and the small dog was all he had left. To some people, that would mean nothing, but to Eric, it meant everything.

"We're going to be okay," Eric said to Pepe. "I promise. Somehow, some way, we'll make it."

Pepe wagged his tail, making Eric smile.

"We'll even go for a walk if there are no zombies around," Eric added.

Pepe wagged his tail even harder at the word *walk* and Eric found himself laughing despite everything.

After shaving, changing into fresh clothes, and a lunch of sandwiches and what was left of the fresh fruit, Eric felt better and a little more clearheaded. His dream, though disturbing, had reminded him that fighting for his life to the bitter end was something he could do.

Being a good Episcopalian, he believed in God and the afterlife. The ruined bodies of the once living did not hold the souls of those poor people. They were just ravaged shells. He had to believe that the souls of his folks, Brandy and Stephanie were in a different place. Free of pain and fear.

But he was still alive and he could fight for that life. He believed that his life had a purpose. He always had. What it was now, in this new dead world, he wasn't sure.

"I feel like Job," he said to Pepe as he finished his strawberries. "Like God is testing me to see if I will curse His name or keep going."

Pepe looked up from where he was chewing on the antique toy. It was pretty much destroyed now, whatever it had been. It had looked like either a cat or weird cow.

"Maybe this is Satan's big plan to take over the world from God," Eric mused. He hadn't really thought about spirituality in a long time. He went to church on occasion with Brandy, but for the big holidays. Though he had remained faithful in his belief in God, other spirits like demons and angels seemed fanciful. Now that the dead walked the earth, he couldn't help but wonder if maybe there was just a bit more to it all than he had considered.

"Maybe all of humanity is Job, being tested by Satan to see if we turn on God." He chewed a blueberry thoughtfully. "Maybe this is some kind of big reset."

Pepe yawned dramatically and flopped next to the ruined doll. He had tinkled in the bathroom again and Eric felt bad for making the dog rough it. He needed to check the perimeter of the house before they ventured out. Clearing the table, he took a deep breath.

Maybe Stephanie had climbed onto the roof. Maybe she had only enough time to type a goodbye before plunging out a window to scramble to safety. Maybe she was already rescued. Of course, she was most likely dead...or undead. Yet that tiny spark of hope that maybe, just maybe, she had escaped made him feel more hopeful about his own situation.

He performed his regular routine before they ventured out: checked out all the windows, off the balcony, studied the view through the peephole, looked at Pepe to see if he was alarmed, then finally opened the door. It was a lovely afternoon and perhaps deceptively calm. Pepe skipped down the walk to find a suitable place to do his business and Eric yawned loudly.

Above birds soared on the spring breeze and the insects buzzed in the garden. It was hard to believe that the world as he knew it had ended.

Once Pepe was done with his business, they walked down to the parking lot together. Eric held the revolver in his hand and had the shotgun slung over his shoulder.

"Okay, boy, are any zombies around?"

Pepe looked back at him, kicked up his back feet, and trotted to the end of his leash. Eric wasn't sure why he trusted the dog so thoroughly, but he felt himself relax as they started down the drive. The walk was uneventful and despite his trepidation, Eric strolled down far enough to take a look through his binoculars at the community center.

Shadow figures lurked inside, but none were in the streets.

"We're still safe," Eric said to Pepe.

The dog skipped along the edge of the road after a bug, ignoring him.

Looking over his shoulder, Eric could see where his car rested in the foliage off the road. In his despair, he had forgotten about the revolver that Brandy had taken with her when she fled. He had the shotgun and the soldier's weapon, but having one more weapon would be beneficial. Dragging Pepe behind him, Eric gingerly maneuvered through the grass and down the slope to the car.

Nervous, he looked back at Pepe to see the dog sniffing the back tire. Rolling his shoulders to work the knots of stress out of his back, he fought against his fear and focused his thoughts.

The car had slammed into the trunks of several trees and was covered in shade. Dappled light played over the shattered glass. Squinting, his eyes adjusted to the gloom and his breath caught in his throat as he saw the speckles of blood shimmering on the broken windshield.

Brandy had died here.

Tears stung his eyes as the glass crunched under his loafers. Leaning slowly through the smashed driver's side window, he could spell the sharp tang of blood, coppery and cloying. It almost made him retch.

Drawing his head back, he took a breath of fresh air before leaning back through the window, careful of the fragments of glass. He was tall and long enough that he could feel under the driver's seat relatively easily.

Nothing.

Pulling his torso out of the car, he tried to pry open the door. It wouldn't budge. Glancing at the dog, he saw that Pepe was watching him with great interest. Walking around to the other side of the car, he pulled on the passenger door. It creaked open.

Pepe woofed softly.

Eric whirled around, his heart beating harshly in his chest.

Pepe leaped into the car and dove into the back seat.

"No, Pepe, we're not going for a ride. The car won't work," Eric said, relief flooding him. He began to search the floorboard for the weapon as Pepe sniffed around the back seat. The glove compartment yielded no sign of the gun either. "What did she do with it?"

The little dog pulled on his leash as he tried to climb into the front seat. Eric was trying very hard not to look at the blood pooled on the seat and on the floor mat. Again, he wondered what had happened to Brandy. At last, he gave up on finding the weapon. Perhaps she had been attacked elsewhere and dropped the gun.

Yanking on the leash, he ordered Pepe to his side as he started to look through the grass around the car. Pepe obediently trotted at his side, craning his head once in awhile to look for the birds stirring in the branches above them.

At last, Eric gave up. His nerves were shot anyway. Being out in the open for so long had every muscle in his body gripped in a vise of tension filled pain. He climbed back to the road and started back.

The stroll was tranquil. Pepe trotted along without a care in the world and Eric felt comforted by that. They were lucky the entire town was locked away in that community center or had taken off to other places to be with their families. He wondered about Mrs. Waskom, but he had a bad feeling about her fate.

Once back inside the house, he locked the door and let Pepe off the leash. The little dog skipped down the hall to the kitchen to take a long drink of water from his bowl. Eric went back to Mrs. Waskom's office and turned on the monitor.

On the screen was another chat message. It wasn't from Stephanie but someone with the tag *Ashley Oaks CitySec.*

The message simply read: *If you're alive, lemme know.*

Eric immediately wrote back: *I'm here. Safe and sound.*

There was a very long pause then more words appeared: *where in texas, hon?*

Eric quickly typed out his location, his hands trembling with excitement and nervousness.

When the words popped up in the box, he let out a breath he didn't realize he was holding.

I'm in Ashley Oaks. We're holed up in city hall and inside a construction site. You're not too far from us. Thirty miles.

Eric quickly typed, explaining his situation and asking if she was safe.

Got lots of people here. Got a wall put up. Got supplies to last awhile. People are off getting guns. Lots of zombies though, hon. Keep where you are til we clear them out.

Eric laughed with delight and quickly typed back that he would do just that, and requested that they let him know when the coast was clear.

We'll come get you when we can. Just gotta kill a whole lot of zombies first. We got a plan to do it and it shouldn't take long.

Pepe skipped into the room with the toy in his mouth and plopped down next to the chair.

"We're not alone, Pepe. There are other people out there and they're safe. They're in a safe place. They actually think they can take out a whole crowd of zombies."

Pepe didn't look too impressed by this and kept chewing on the doll.

Eric looked back at the screen. The words that glowed there made him feel a little less alone in the ugliness of the world.

The words read: *My name is Peggy. And I'm glad to meet ya.*

12.
Clones, Aliens and Amazons

Hope is a wondrous thing. After typing back and forth with Peggy most of the afternoon, the malaise and depression that had threatened to overwhelm Eric shrank back from the glory of his newfound hope.

Before his conversation with Peggy he had decided to fight for his life and Pepe's, but after realizing that there were more survivors out there, he felt a renewed sense of community and drew strength from it. He wasn't alone. There were others. And they had a place saved for him in their *fort.*

That night, he actually made himself dinner instead of eating a sandwich or leftovers. Using the last of the fresh vegetables and thawing out some chicken, he made a meal that left him feeling sated and a little more normal.

Afterward, he sat upstairs in his room with a cup of coffee and the last piece of pie. Bored and curious to see if anything was changing, he began flipping through the TV channels one by one. The major networks were gone and running the emergency broadcast feed. It was looping the same old news. All the other cable networks were gone now.

Channel after channel, there was nothing but static.

Pepe trotted into the room dragging the nearly destroyed toy and flung it down in front of the TV to continue its mutilation. Eric grinned and leaned down to pet Pepe's head as he continued to flip channels.

"...and they knew it..."

His finger automatically hit the channel button despite hearing the voice. He quickly hit the return button. An old man's face filled the screen, a craggy face with a big nose and deep wrinkles in the sun worn flesh. His eyes were wide and very intense under his wiry eyebrows and he wore what appeared to be an army helmet with foil glued to it.

"...think it's coincidence that the President was at Camp David and the VP was out in East Texas hunting when this all went down? I tell you no! No, no, no, no! How many stories did they use to cover up the truth? Stories about people biting each other? Or killing so they could...could..." The old guy backed away from the screen and he pantomimed a zombie eating a person quite well. *"You know...eat!"*

"Whoa, what a crazy old geezer," Eric said in awe.

The old man was standing in the middle of a long, narrow room that appeared to be made of cement blocks and concrete. There was a cot in one corner piled with blankets and pillows, a very beat-up sofa was filled with all sorts of dogs that were watching the old man with rapt attention, and a table was shoved up along one wall and full of computer and electronic equipment.

"So they covered it all up. Hid it. Pretended they didn't fuck up the clones and that the clones got out and started eating people. Cause the clones were all fucked up!" The old guy pointed to his head and then leaned close to the camera again. *"All fucked up in the head. And you know why?"*

Eric and Pepe looked at each other then back at the TV.

"Aliens."

"I kinda knew he was going that way," Eric said.

Pepe barked in agreement.

"They're making deals with the Amazonian queen. They want this planet. They want its resources. So by letting those clones out, they get what they want. And you know what I say?" The old man leaned closer to the camera so only his mouth full of gnarled teeth was showing. At the top of his lungs, he shouted, *"Fuck you, aliens!"*

Eric fell back against the bed and began to laugh.

The old guy looked quite indignant and a cat sauntered up to the camera and looked into it for a long moment, then walked on. Once the screen was clear of the cat, the old guy came into view sitting at his mish-mash of equipment.

"I'm watching them, survivors. Oh, yeah. I'm watching them. I know what's going on. I can't keep broadcasting forever to you 'cause they'll find me sooner or later, but I'm telling you, I got my eye on them. Oh, yeah," he said reassuringly.

Suddenly the lights in the bunker turned bright red as an alarm started to peal.

"Gawddamn clones!"

The old guy sprang to his feet, ran to the camera, picked it up and ran back to his desk. Propping up the camera so it was filming what appeared to be a security monitor, the old guy's long dirty finger came into view as he pointed out what was happening.

"See, there come the clones again. Always coming up on the east side of my property. I'm telling you, they know where I am. And they're sending their damn messed up clones."

On the screen a bunch of the dead were pushing against a barbwire fence.

"Hate those guys," the old guy muttered as he pointed to each zombie individually on the monitor. *"All screwed up and spilling guts on my land."*

Though Eric couldn't see what he was doing, he could hear the old man typing away on a keyboard.

To his amazement, on the monitor screen what looked like some sort of makeshift robotic arm made out of farm equipment rose out of a haystack and opened fire on the zombies with an Uzi.

"Gawdamn clones," the old man was muttering angrily. *"Good thing I got my security system up before it all went to shit. And that is where they fucked us, didn't they? They didn't tell us they were out there. The clones. Doing what they do. They hid it 'cause that's what they were supposed to do. But I knew! I knew!"*

The camera continued to film the scene on the monitor as the robotic arm swept back and forth with the Uzi strafing anything standing outside the fence. In just a few short minutes, all the zombies were dead.

"Gotta go, kiddies. Gotta go put more ammo in the Uzi. Gotta keep alert. Don't let the government do nothing for ya. Don't go to those rescue shelters. Keep hiding. Stock up on food and ammo, cause boys and girls, them clones are doing the work of the Amazonian Queen and her alien overlords and we gotta be ready to fight back." The old guy swiveled the camera so his face filled the screen again. *"Calhoun, over and out."*

The screen switched to what looked like a cardboard box that had the words " The Truth is Here" written in magic marker on it.

Eric sat on the floor in stunned silence for a few seconds then began to howl with laughter. He didn't stop for a long time.

13.
Taking Risks

The hope that was born in Eric when he first made communication with the survivors in Ashley Oaks, Texas, grew each day as his surroundings remained zombie free. It was an enormous relief to know that pockets of humanity were still surviving. Even though the phones were down in the area of the fort, the Internet was still working via the cable lines. Peggy explained that they had a communication center up where they were talking to survivors over CBs and ham radios as well as the Internet.

He enjoyed talking to Peggy. She was obviously the town gossip and had all the news about what was going on in the fort. As they chatted on and off during the day, she started to feel like a friend. Yet he was still lonely. He longed for human interaction and it was hard not to miss Brandy.

Even though he had a renewed sense of hope, at times he felt overwhelmed with the loss of Brandy and his family. He kept trying to call his family, but no one ever answered at his sister or brother's place. The phone's busy signal at his parents' house told a tragic story he did not want to ponder. A few messages from old school chums were posted on his Facebook page, but most of them were holed up and fighting to survive. The questions on the boards and chat rooms for survivors were the same.

Was the army coming soon?

How long before FEMA would open secure shelters?

Was the government up and running?

Was anyone getting updated news reports in their area?

He watched Calhoun's regular broadcasts every night while eating dinner. The old guy always rambled on about clones, aliens and Amazons, but he was highly amusing. His instructional video on how to kill a zombie was fairly disgusting, but darkly humorous at the same time.

"Cutting off their arm does you no damn good if they got their other arm," Calhoun said at one point during the demonstration. He danced around a zombie caught in the barbed wire fence surrounding his property as chickens and a dog wandered around the moaning, hungry zombie. *"See?"* Calhoun whacked off one arm with a machete and the zombie kept reaching with the hand. *"It still got the other one to get ya. You gotta smack 'em in da damn head."* With a deft whack of the machete, the zombie was no more.

"Public access was never this exciting back in the old days," Eric decided, looking down at Pepe who was still hell-bent on destroying the antique toy.

The dog eyeballed him, then went back to gnawing.

The next day, Eric made sure to find a machete in the barn and rig a holster so he could hang it on his belt.

Every day he took Pepe on a walk. If Pepe was calm and not bothered by their surroundings, Eric felt confident that they were safe to take a walk down the road to the accident site where Brandy had died. It bothered Eric, but the location allowed him to clearly see the community center.

Despite the danger that he knew lurked nearby, he grew bolder as the zombies remained contained to the community center.

One day he finally accepted he was going to have to make a supply run. The pantry was down to a few cans and a lot of the food in the refrigerator was starting to go bad.

"We're going to have to go shopping," he decided.

Pepe burrowed into the bottom of the dog food bag. With a sigh, Eric leaned down to pull him out. He would have to refresh Pepe's supply from the kennels.

Making sure he was well-armed, his machete at his side, his gun tucked into his waistband, and the shotgun looped over his shoulder, he leashed Pepe. After making sure there were none of the undead wandering around outside, he slipped out the back door and hurried around the house to the ATV. Pepe sniffed at the ground as they strode to the vehicle, showing no sign of alarm.

Relieved, Eric started climbed onto the ATV. He was wearing a lightweight windbreaker and tucked the dog into it. Pepe immediately popped his head out, his tail tickling Eric's belly as it wagged with excitement.

Driving down the road toward town, Eric was again struck with how peaceful the world appeared. The birds continued to sing, the insects hummed, squirrels darted along the branches of the trees, and an occasional deer wandered into view. Though the noises of nature were soothing to his ears, the eerie lack of the sounds of humanity made him shiver. He sometimes felt like he was the last person left alive. If not for his communication with Peggy, he might have believed it.

Riding along the curve of the road, the ATV sped past his crashed car. Pulling over, he tugged his binoculars out of his jacket pocket and took a look at the community center.

Figures still shifted behind the blood-stained windows. There was no sign that any had escaped.

"Okay, here we go."

The ATV skirted around the field before turning toward town. The convenience store he had visited before the world had died was his destination. Pepe watched the world fly by, the wind ruffling his ears. A few times his head perked up, his ears shifting upward, his body alert, and each time, Eric's body tensed. But Pepe didn't bark, just relaxed back into the jacket.

The empty road and sidewalks were a chilling sight as were the Closed signs tucked into the front door or window of all the businesses. Nervously, Eric pulled up in front of the store and glanced warily toward the community center. He started to lift his binoculars, but stopped himself. This close he would be able to see the true terror of what lay beyond those windows and barricaded doors.

Climbing off the four-wheeler, Eric set Pepe on the sidewalk, looping the end of the leash over his wrist. The dog trotted along beside him as Eric pulled the blue tarp covering the trailer. An ax was wedged along the side and he yanked it out. Checking on his dog, he saw that the terrier was alert, but did not seem alarmed. Sweeping his gaze over the street, he tried to steady the shaking of his hands. He would make this quick and get back to the farmhouse.

Striding to the door to the convenience store, he started to lift the ax, but thought better of it. Reaching out, he pulled on the door latch. It resisted.

Motioning Pepe back, he lifted the ax and slammed it into the glass inset in the door. It shattered and crashed to the sidewalk. Pepe uttered a startled yelp.

Fearful, Eric swung around, studying his surroundings again. Nothing stirred in the street except a squirrel dashing to a nearby tree. Sweat running down his face, he waited next to the door, his ears straining to hear if anything stirred inside. Silence answered him. Carefully, he reached through the broken glass edging the window and turned the lock inside. The door swung open.

Eric took a cautious step inside, Pepe at his side. The dog sniffed at the air, then looked up at Eric expectantly.

"I guess that means we're clear, huh?"

Eric moved further into the gloom filling the convenience store, clutching the ax in his hands. The wood floor creaked and the shattered glass crunched under the heels of his loafers. The refrigeration units at the back were silent and dark. The radio was quiet behind the old counter.

Fabric shopping bags with the name of the town hung on a hook beside the cash register and Eric grabbed the whole lot of them. He hurried into one of the aisles and dropped the ax on the floor. Moving swiftly, he began to pack each one with all the canned goods, snacks, and first aid supplies he could find. Pepe watched him with a solemn expression on his face, occasionally glancing toward the front door.

Sweat beaded and slid down his forehead into his eyes. In the murk dwelling in the store, he felt vulnerable and afraid. He tried to keep an eye on the entrance as he worked. After each bag was filled, he set it next to the door. As he swept candy into the last bag, he lamented the sorry state of his future diet, but he couldn't be picky. At last, he stacked several 12-packs of water next to the bags.

Muscles aching, head throbbing, heart harshly beating, Eric fought down his growing panic. Every shadow made him jump, every noise scared him. He had seen enough scary movies over his lifetime to expect a monster to come lurching out at him at any moment. The only zombie movie he had ever seen was the original *Night of the Living Dead*. He couldn't imagine how terrifying it would be to look out into the street and see the mindless dead shambling around. Instead, they were cloistered in the nearby community center. If he and Pepe were lucky, maybe they would never escape. The town was far enough from any highway or other town that maybe no zombies would ever show up here.

Shaking his head, he pushed those thoughts away. He was stalling for time and he knew it. Once he stepped out the door, he would be in clear view of any zombie that might be wandering around. Hurrying back to the aisle, he grabbed the ax and headed to the door.

"Okay, Pepe, keep a lookout," he told the dog.

Pepe stared intently at the door, waiting for it to open.

Checking out the front windows one more time, Eric swung the door open and hurried out to the trailer. First he stowed the ax away, then rushed back to grab the bags. Darting back and forth between the trailer and the store, he took deep breaths as he tried not to panic. Pepe stood in the center of the sidewalk staring down the road toward the community center as Eric worked.

Eric had just loaded the last of the water bottles onto the trailer and was securing the tarp when Pepe let out a low growl. Chills flowed over Eric's scalp and down his spine. Whipping about, he drew his gun. Pepe lowered his head, the growl intensifying. Panicked, Eric scurried back to the ATV and dragged the dog behind him.

"Come on, Pepe!"

Eric yanked the dog off the ground by his harness and shoved him into his jacket. Pepe began to bark wildly, twisting around to look over Eric's shoulder. With shaking hands, Eric drew the revolver and rotating in the seat, he aimed in the direction he had come from earlier.

It took a few seconds for the roar of the truck to penetrate the buzzing in his rattled mind. A massive monster truck broke into view from a side road. He briefly glimpsed a woman wearing sunglasses behind the wheel before she turned the big truck with flames painted on the side onto the road that would lead her past the turn-off to the bed and breakfast. Dust blew across the road in the path of the vehicle as it roared out of town. Pepe was barking so loud it hurt Eric's ears.

"Wait!" Eric shouted, recovering his senses. Turning on the ATV, he pulled it around and raced after the vehicle, excitement filling him. He wasn't alone. Dry leaves, dirt, and dust blew into his face as he tried to follow in the truck's wake. "Come back!"

Eric doubted the woman driving the truck could hear him, let alone see him. Pepe continued to bark as the truck sped away and finally vanished over a hill.

Slowing down, Eric felt the sudden burst of hope he had felt when he first saw the truck dissipate like vapor. Swerving onto the road that would lead back to the house, Eric kissed the top of Pepe's head gently.

"It's just you and me, boy," he said in a sad voice. "Just you and me."

14.
An Unexpected Turn

"Travis and Katie are due back tomorrow with the guns," Eric said to Pepe one day as they took their walk. "Peggy says they went to Ralph's store to get more ammunition and they are coming back tomorrow because Juan corralled all the zombies somehow so they can get in. That means we can get in soon, too."

Pepe glanced up at him nonchalantly as he trotted along.

Speaking of the people he would soon meet was reassuring and made him feel less alone. "Peggy says this girl named Jenni got all the zombies to move to one spot on the road and they dropped containers down to make this t-shaped corral so Travis and Katie can drive in safely on the other side of the containers." Eric paused, trying to imagine this in his mind. "Not quite sure how that works, but it sounds interesting."

The names came easily to him. He imagined faces behind the names and wondered what it would feel like to be a part of that community. Peggy seemed positive that once the zombies were cleared out around the fort someone would come out to get him and Pepe. Though the conditions were not as nice as the farmhouse, the fort sounded much safer. He was more than willing to rough it to be behind the walls of the fort. Besides, Peggy said there was a massive old-fashioned hotel to one side of the fort they were planning on occupying in the near future.

Pepe tugged harder on his leash as they neared the curve in the road and Eric hurried to catch up with the little dog. Alarmingly, Pepe started to bark loudly and fiercely. With his heart lurching in his chest, Eric immediately pulled out the revolver and flicked the safety off. As they reached the end of the tree line and the field separating them from the town came into view, Eric felt his throat constrict.

Running across the field were two men and one woman. The trio shouted at each other to run faster as they raced toward him. They were quite a distance away so he could barely make out their expressions of terror. Behind them was a large crowd of the dead. The less mutilated ones were fast on their feet, rushing after the living, while the brutally mauled ones staggered and stumbled behind.

Eric could barely breathe as he raised his binoculars to view the spot he was so used to checking every day. The community center swam into view. The dead were pouring out of an open window and a few were clustered over fresh bodies shoving bits of flesh into their mouths.

He dropped his binoculars and they painfully banged against his chest.

"Oh, shit," he exclaimed as the enormity of what was happening hit him.

With Pepe snarling and barking at his heels, he ran up the hill back toward the house.

15.
Racing Death

Eric ran up past the edge of the tree line and into the shade of the leafy boughs hanging over the drive. He could hear the moans and howls of the undead and the shouts of the living behind him.

"Help!" he heard the woman's voice screaming in the distance.

He hesitated and Pepe pulled insistently on the leash urging Eric on. Eric felt tears well in his eyes. His first impulse had been to run, but those people were alive and he could help them.

But what if they had been bitten?

He hesitantly began to walk back toward the open field, but Pepe pulled on the leash and barked at him. He stopped abruptly and took a deep breath.

Pepe was right. He had to survive. Eric's hand tightened on the revolver as he decided to run back to the safety of the bed and breakfast.

"Help!" the woman shouted again.

This time her voice was much closer. Eric turned back in surprise. She sprinted onto the road at an amazing speed. Dressed in athletic shorts and a tank top with the word *Coach* written on it, she was petite and muscular with deeply tanned skin and pale blond hair pulled back in a ponytail.

"Please help!"

Despite Pepe's snarls and persistent tugging on the leash, Eric stood and waited for her.

"Hurry!" he yelled.

"Coop and Sean are right behind me," she called out. "Just run!"

"Right!"

Eric bolted up the road as fast as he could, wishing he had worn something other than loafers. He was not as fit as the woman racing up the road behind him. He struggled to find a rhythm in his out of shape gait. Frantically, he tried to regulate his breath and find a fast, steady pace. He was just finding a steady beat to his breathing and his speed when, to his surprise, the young woman caught up with him. Her breath was not nearly as ragged as his was already becoming.

"Do you have shelter? A place for us to go? Is the farmhouse ok?"

"Yeah," Eric huffed. "Yeah. That's where I've been."

"Keep running!" a voice shouted behind them.

Eric glanced back long enough to see an older man, also incredibly fit and also in a coach's uniform, and younger man clad in jeans and a T-shirt, coming up over the embankment and onto the road far behind them. The girl ran faster than he did and she took the lead with her short ponytail bouncing behind her and her toned arms pumping hard.

Eric struggled to keep moving at a quick pace despite the burning in his calves and his breath flowing short and hard into his lungs. Walking up the hill had been moderate exercise the last few days, but running was a whole other story.

The young woman hesitated in her steps to look back and again the man's voice rang out, "Keep running."

Eric looked back again to see both men gaining on him. More terrifying was that so were the fast, blood covered creatures behind the men. He had a vague impression of football uniforms and what was maybe army fatigues under all the blood and gore. The zombies hadn't done much damage to what appeared to be the more physically fit people in the community center. Terrified by what he saw, Eric ran harder and tried to gain speed. Pepe scampered ahead of him, almost to the end of his leash, his nails clicking against the asphalt.

"The door is unlocked," Eric choked out to the girl running in front of him. He realized with her quick pace she would get there first. He was beginning to doubt he would make it with his body feeling like it was about to explode.

The girl tossed a look over her shoulder, nodded and sprinted across the gardens toward the safety of the bed and breakfast. Eric followed in her wake, but he was now breathless and struggling to keep his exhausted limbs moving. The blond woman reached the porch, jumped over the steps, effortlessly ran across the whitewashed wood and shoved the front door open.

Following in her footsteps, Eric leaped onto the end of the porch and felt his legs quiver. They almost buckled under him, but he forced himself to keep moving.

"Get in! Get in!"

Again the older man's voice shouted out from behind him. It sounded much closer now: as did the growls and howls of the dead. Eric's feet pounded across the wood porch as Pepe strained at the end of his leash to get into the house.

Eric caught the edge of the doorway with his hand and hurled his body inside. The girl was standing in the shadows of the foyer with her hand on the door, ready to shove it shut. Pepe whipped around and began to bark wildly at the open door.

Eric barely managed not to collapse, gasping for breath. He heard footfalls on the porch and the girl tensed.

"We're almost there!" another man's voice shouted. "Keep it open!"

Eric stared at the doorway in terror as he listened to the sound of more feet leaping onto the porch. The two men suddenly filled the doorway and jostled each other getting into the house. Once they both cleared the entry, the girl shoved the door closed. It was stopped by the ghastly, bloody stump of an arm that was shoved into the gap just before the door shut.

"No!" Her voice was raw with terror.

The older man immediately turned and shoved his shoulder into the door, bracing his feet. More hands, some missing fingers, all covered in blood, shoved into the gap trying to reach the living people within the house. The second man, his shirt splattered in blood, also braced his shoulder against the door as it vibrated under the pounding onslaught of the zombies. Eric lurched forward and placed his hands on the wood and shoved it. Just beyond the barrier of wood and leaded glass, the dead moaned hungrily and Eric could feel the door beginning to move inward.

"Push harder!" the older man ordered.

"Coop," the girl sobbed in terror, "they're coming in!"

Pepe darted up the stairs, his leash dragging behind him and Eric felt a moment of panic for his little companion. The dog stopped at the first landing and barked down at him.

Straining to lock his legs in place and shove the door shut, Eric looked up at Pepe feeling overwhelmed with the futility of it all. Pepe barked one more time, looked at the slowly opening door, then raced up the stairs.

"It's still opening," Sean, the younger man, exclaimed, his dark eyes flashing with fear.

"I got an ATV out back with a trailer hitched to it. We can escape on that," Eric blurted out.

The door pushed in another inch as more dead reached the house and joined their brethren in assaulting the door.

"Go, Stacey!" Coop ordered.

"Dad!"

"Go! Go with him!"

Eric let out a gasp as he felt the door sliding inward another inch. "The back door opens up to face the road. They'll see us. But the fire escape slide upstairs will put us on the other side of the house away from them!"

"Stacey, go!" Sean yelled at her. "We'll hold the door!"

The young woman looked at him with a terrible expression that broke Eric's heart.

"Dad, Sean..."

"Go!" The older man groaned as more hands shoved past the yawning door. "Go! Sean and I will follow."

Stacey stared at Coop and Sean with tears in her eyes. She kissed the older man's cheek and grabbed Eric's hand.

"Let's go!"

Her slick, clammy fingers in his, Eric bolted up the stairs, pulling her along behind him.

"Brace it, brace it!" Coop's voice ordered as Eric heard the door scrape open a little further.

Together, Eric and Stacey reached the second floor and ran down the hallway. Eric was relieved to see Pepe waiting for him at the window with the fire escape ladder. He unlatched the window and shoved it open as Stacey yanked the slide out of its box and hooked it over the windowsill. The slide was barely in place when she ripped the cord and it inflated.

Without hesitation, Stacey heaved herself out the window and slipped down the slide to the ground below. She immediately sprang to her feet and dashed to the waiting ATV. Eric snatched Pepe up into his arms and followed her. He gasped as he slid down far more quickly than he had anticipated, and almost didn't catch himself as his feet hit the ground.

Ahead of him, Stacey reached the ATV and straddled the seat. He ran with Pepe in his arms and was relieved to see her twist the key he always kept in the ignition.

"I'll drive," he said, thrusting Pepe into her arms.

She hastily slid back on the seat to make room for Eric. Holding down the brake, he quickly turned the killswitch on and hit the starter. The engine grumbled to life and he gripped the handlebars tightly.

"You can't wait to let it warm up!" Stacey looked back toward the house as tears streamed down her face. "Just go."

Eric nodded, yanked on the accelerator and the ATV lurched forward. He aimed it toward the route he had already planned. Of course, he hadn't anticipated anyone being with him. Sweat was pouring into his eyes and his heart was thudding so hard it felt like it was about to explode, he drove the vehicle away from the house alongside the fenced-in pasture.

"Wait!"

It was a desperately barked out word.

Stacey looked back as Eric hit the brake.

Sean was at the window.

"He's still alive!" Stacey almost dropped Pepe in surprise. "Hurry, Sean!"

Eric grabbed Pepe from Stacey's grasp and shoved him into his light jacket and zipped it up.

In a panic, the young man flung himself out onto the slide as greedy dead hands grabbed for him. He landed on the slide too far to one side and he fell off. The zombies scrambled out the window after him. A few slid down the slide to land hard on the ground, while a few others fell near Sean.

"Get up! Get up!" Stacey's voice was shrill.

Sean managed to get to his feet and deftly avoided the grasp of the zombies lunging toward him. Hobbled by his fall, he rushed toward the ATV, dragging his one leg behind him. The zombies continued to fall out of the window and land on the ground. A few busted their heads open against the flagstone pathway or broke their necks on impact. The zombies sliding down to the ground piled up in a heap of twisting arms and legs. Luckily, they didn't seem to know how to untangle themselves and get up.

Sean was almost to the ATV when some faster, fiercer zombies rounded the corner of the house.

"We gotta go!" Eric exclaimed, pulling on the accelerator again and the ATV lurched forward.

There was no time to wait for Sean and they both knew it.

With an unbelievable amount of willpower, Sean pushed his body to the limit despite his pain and managed to throw himself onto the trailer behind the ATV. The hands of the pursuing zombies grabbed for him and one or two managed to snag his clothes. Sean twisted his body in an attempt to get free from the grasping creatures and shouted for Eric to go faster. He kicked his legs to dislodge the zombies while trying to hold onto the edge of the trailer.

"Sean! Sean!" Stacey's arms were painfully tight around Eric's waist and she screamed as one of the zombies dove onto the trailer as the ATV gained speed.

The scarily fast, still fresh zombie tried to use its handhold on Sean's shirt to pull itself onto the trailer. Sean managed to get one foot on the creature's chest and kicked it off him. It tumbled away into the high grass as the ATV turned onto the dirt road that led into the wooded hills.

"He made it," she gasped with relief. "He made it!"

Eric kept his gaze steady on the road ahead. He wasn't sure if he felt relief or not. His body was tight with fear and frustration. He felt Pepe squirming around in his jacket and took a deep breath to steady his nerves and his hands. The dog poked his head out of the collar of the jacket and Eric felt the comforting softness of the dog's fur underneath his chin.

Stacey laid her head against his shoulder and he could feel her body shuddering with her sobs. In the rear view mirrors, Eric saw the more fleet-footed zombies trying to chase after them, but slowly they began to drop away as the ATV rode faster up the dirt road and away from the bed and breakfast that had been his safe haven. Behind them, on the trailer, Sean curled up in a tight ball, exhausted and overwhelmed.

"Where are we going?" Stacey finally asked.

"I don't know," Eric answered.

16.
War Stories

As the ATV grumbled up the dirt road dragging the overloaded flat trailer behind it, Eric took deep breaths trying to soothe his frazzled nerves. He hoped it would bring his heart rate down so it wouldn't feel like it was about to burst out of his chest.

Stacey clung to him, her head still on his shoulder, her sobs fading as she gained control. They were both soaked in sweat and the warm breeze did nothing to soothe their hot flesh. Pepe adjusted himself so he could rest his chin on the edge of the jacket collar and snuggle against Eric. His little heart had been racing, too, and Eric could feel the small dog slowly relaxing.

"I don't see any following," Stacey said in his ear. Her voice sounded ragged with emotion.

Eric checked his mirrors again. The roof of bed and breakfast was dropping away from view behind the treetops as the ATV climbed the hill. He still couldn't believe his safe haven had been destroyed. It had happened so quickly it didn't seem real. How he could have ever believed that he could stay in relative comfort until the rescue team arrived? In this world, nothing was truly safe or stable.

"Can we stop? My brother is in a lot of pain." Stacey's voice was very strained.

Eric shook his head. "Not until we crest the hill. Not until we're out of sight of for sure. I don't want to risk us, okay?"

He glanced into the rearview mirror on his right side and noticed she had turned to gaze at the form on the trailer. Returning her gaze forward, she caught sight of his reflection in the mirror. Their gaze met in the reflective glass. She slowly nodded and lowered her eyes.

Eric could see her brother, Sean, lying in what appeared to be a very uncomfortable position on the blue plastic tarp Eric had used to cover the boxed up supplies. He directed his attention back to the dirt road as they climbed higher. The trees thinned out as they traveled. One side sloped down to reveal the colorful carpet of wildflowers in the pasture far below. At last they crested the hill and the amazing panorama of the Texas Hill Country came into view.

Again, Eric was struck by both the beauty and deadliness of the day.

Pulling over to the side of the road, Eric shifted gears and the ATV grumbled low as it idled. Stacey immediately slid off the vehicle and ran to the trailer. Eric followed, unzipping his jacket and pulling Pepe free. The Jack Russell Terrier looked around with interest, but did not fall into a barking fit. Eric took it as a good sign. He set Pepe on the ground and slid the loop of the leash onto his wrist.

Pepe immediately began sniffing the tires, the ground, his shoes, and Stacey's sneakers.

Stacey leaned over her brother and he awoke with a start. For a second he didn't recognize her and drew back sharply, and then he realized where they were and relaxed.

"We made it?"

"Yeah, Sean. We made it. But you're pretty banged up," Stacey answered, relief slowly filling her voice. "We need to stop the bleeding..." Her hand hovered over his bloodied arm.

"What happened?" Eric untied some of the rope holding the blue tarp in place and fumbled for the first aid kit.

"To get out of the community center, we had to bust out one of those damn extra thick Plexiglas windows," Sean explained, wincing as his sister studied his still bleeding wounds. "Who makes windows five inches thick? That was freaking crazy."

"I only saw dead things through the windows. Where were you guys?" Eric pulled open the big tin box.

Stacey grabbed up some cotton and alcohol.

Sean winced as his sister began to clean up his wounds. "Well, there is an office block in the back. It's where the Chamber of Commerce folks were. There are these huge old metal doors between that area and the Community Center. We've been on the Chamber of Commerce side," Sean explained.

"So you couldn't get out?" Eric asked.

"Nope. They chained all the doors shut." Sean gasped as his sister applied pressure to staunch the bleeding of his wounds.

"To keep us safe," Stacey said sourly.

Eric handed Stacey some gauze and she took it gratefully. Her fingers were red with her brother's blood and Eric felt a little lightheaded by the sight. It made him think of all the blood in the car where Brandy had died.

"Watch it, Stacey! That hurts! So we couldn't get out once it went bad. The Sheriff had the keys and he was the first one down when those...those..."

"Zombies," Eric offered helpfully.

Eric could see the disbelief in Sean's eyes at the sound of the word despite all he had witnessed. Slowly, Sean nodded. "Yeah, zombies. The soldiers from the crash and some of the rescue guys were mauled by one of the...we thought he was just crazed from his injuries...one of the survivors of the crash. They were being treated in the main room of the community center and the Sheriff was questioning the pilot when suddenly one of the soldiers just got up off his bunk and bit into the Sheriff's face."

Stacey grimaced at the memory and lifted the gauze to check the wound. It was still bleeding. "It went bad fast."

"Real fast," Sean agreed. "About half those wounded guys started getting up and attacking people. Then those people started attacking people."

"And we were trying to get out but the doors were chained." Stacey shook her head. "So my Dad and another guy started herding everyone toward the office area. It was a mad crush and..." Stacey faltered. She shrugged and continued to press down hard on her flinching brother's arm.

"How many got into the office area?"

"Twenty-three," Sean answered softly. His dark eyes glittered with tears. "Two died of wounds and..."

"Got up. Coop bashed their brains in with a fire extinguisher."

"Your dad?" Eric swallowed hard thinking of the strong older man who had sacrificed himself at the house.

"Yeah. Everyone, even us, called him Coop. He's the town football hero and the coach of the Blazing Riders high school football team," Stacey faltered. "Or...he was."

"He gave his life for us to get away," Sean said to his sister, laying his hand over hers. "He held them off on the stairs so I could get up to the fire slide. He was brave until the end."

"I know." Stacey blinked and tears fell down her dirty cheeks. "I know. But I'd rather have him here."

Sean nodded and was unashamed of his own tears. "He just wanted us to live."

Eric looked down at Pepe who was sniffing around the edge of the trailer. "I...lost someone, too."

"Yeah, well, we lost the whole damn town we grew up in," Stacey snapped and gave him a hard look. "The whole damn town."

Her brother reached out to calm her and she sniffled loudly.

Eric felt sickened by his own selfishness and sat down on the edge of the trailer. "I'm sorry. Really. I am." He looked at her apologetically. "I know seeing so many die is horrible and..."

Stacey shook her head. "I'm sorry. I have no right to snap at you. We've all lost so much."

Eric let out a slow breath. "I didn't know anyone was alive in the community center. If I had known, I would have tried to rescue you."

"How could you know we were there?" Sean shrugged. "Don't feel guilty."

"When did it all go wrong?" Eric stared at his dirty nails and tried not to think too hard about Brandy.

"The first night we were in there, believe it or not. The Sheriff rounded up everyone that had not left town into the community center," Stacey answered. "After we barricaded ourselves into the offices, we lived off the vending machine and the lunches the staff put in the refrigerator in the cafeteria."

"Coop kept trying to get us out, but the Sheriff had us locked in real good. All these heavy damn storm doors chained shut. Super thick windows...we started on one of the windows and it took forever to chip through that stuff."

"Built during the cold war. I think they thought it was A-bomb proof." Stacey rolled her eyes. She peeked at Sean's arm and looked satisfied. Reaching out for the first aid kit, she gave Eric a slight smile.

He felt she was trying to apologize for earlier so he smiled back.

"We were almost through when those things finally breached our barricade. We locked ourselves in the office where we were chipping away at the window and it was a race to get the glass busted out in time. Once the opening was big enough, we started evacuating. The plan had been to go to the high school and get into a school bus, but it was just a crazed scramble at the end." Sean winced and made a terrible face as his sister dressed his wounded arm. The deeper wound was no longer trickling blood and the smaller wounds appeared to have stopped bleeding. "The football players tried to hold the door shut."

Eric flashed back on the mad pursuit up the hill. The fastest of the undead had seemed very fresh and looked like football players. "Oh. Wow."

"Yeah. We evacuated the old people, the women and the kids first. But those things got in and were already..." Sean lowered his head and rubbed his eyes. "They were..."

"Coop realized what was happening and shoved me out the window. Sean was trying to help and our dad told him to get out just as a bunch of them busted in through the damn wall! Some added on modern wall made of cheap materials. Their weight must have done it in." Stacey's hands were shaking as she slowly wrapped her brother's arm.

"Dad and I were the last ones out. Some of them grabbed for me and I did this crazy dive out the window and fucked up my arm." Sean shook his head. "We got outside and Coop was trying to get everyone rallied together when those fast ones started coming out the window after us. Coop shouted for everyone to run. And those still alive..."

"We ran," Stacey said in a tremulous voice. "We ran. But they ran us down. The fast ones. The new ones. The ran down the old folks, the...the...the... kids..." Stacey let out a strangled sob and turned away from Eric and Sean. Her shoulders trembled as she sniffled loudly trying to regain her composure.

Sean reached out to stroke her back gently. "It just...we tried...there was really nothing to use as a weapon. I tried to shove a few of them off this one kid..." He shook his head as more tears flowed. "Coop always made me and Stacey run with him every night. We used to do sprints for fun. He got us into marathon running. Hell, Stacey was a college track star. That's the only reason we were able to keep ahead." Sean looked at Eric with a tormented expression on his face. "We couldn't do anything for the rest. We just ran."

"Coop told us to run to Mrs. Waskom's place, so we did. Then we saw you." Stacey began to run her hands lightly down her brother's leg he had hurt leaping from the window. "And you pretty much know the rest."

"I'm sorry about Coop," Eric said sympathetically. "He seemed so strong."

"He was. He was the best." Stacey's lips turned up in a slight, proud smile even though tears lingered in the corners of her eyes.

Sean winced and let out a small cry as his sister's hands examined his leg.

"I'm guessing a couple of fractures. Which you probably fucked up more by that crazy sprint," Stacey lightly chided Sean.

"Yeah, but I'm here, ain't I?" Sean grinned before grimacing again.

Suddenly Pepe's head shot up and his ears perked. He let out a tentative *woof*.

"I think it's time to go." Eric pointed at Pepe. "He always alerts me when the zombies are around.

Stacey shoved the first aid kit back under the tarp. "Sean, you hold on tight."

"Damn bossy twin sister," Sean grumbled. "Just cause you were born first by two minutes..."

Eric could tell it was an old argument, and Stacey seemed to relax a little at her brother's teasing.

An inhuman howl of hunger echoed across the hillside.

"They're following. We need to go!" Eric swept his snarling dog into his arms.

"Dammit!" Stacey scrabbled onto the ATV.

After Eric was situated behind the handlebars, he felt her arms lock around his waist. With trembling hands, he shoved Pepe into his jacket.

"You guys! Hurry it up!" Sean shouted. "I can see them!"

Casting a quick glance over his shoulder, Eric saw the first of the running zombies cresting the hill.

"Seriously, let's go!" Sean's voice was panicked. "Those things bite hard!"

Eric shifted gears. The ATV roared and sped down the other side of the hill toward the county road in the distance.

"Where are we going?" Stacey's voice was close to his ear and he could feel her body pressing against his back.

"A construction site in Ashley Oaks is being built into a fort. They said they planned a safe way to approach it. I'm gonna try and find it." Eric looked into the rearview mirror and saw the bloodied dead following them down the hill. "Dammit. Those guys do not give up."

Stacey tightened her arms around him. "Just keep going. At the rate they're going they'll blow out their joints at some point. That'll slow them down."

"Trust me," Eric said in a resolute tone. "I'm not stopping until we're safe."

"Or out of gas." Stacey sounded fearful.

"Got spare gasoline in the trailer," Eric assured her.

She was silent for a few minutes. He felt her head rest on his shoulder. It was rather comforting. Finally, her voice said, "Coop liked to be well-prepared. He would have liked you."

Eric smiled slightly at this comment and was surprised when he felt his eyes welling up. "Yeah, I think I would have liked him, too."

As the sun slowly began its descent across the Texas sky, the ATV roared on down the dirt road and the dead followed.

17.
On the Road

The drive to the country road was tense, but uneventful. If the zombies were still pursuing them, they had fallen far enough behind to be out of sight. Eric maneuvered the ATV onto the paved road the dirt trail intersected. The smooth surface was a relief to their weary joints.

Stacey worriedly glanced behind her. She was obviously very worried about her twin. In the review mirror, Eric could see Sean was either asleep or unconscious. Eric worried about how much blood he had lost. There was no way they could go to a hospital or clinic.

"My brother looks so pale."

"He lost a lot of blood. He needs to rest." Eric wasn't certain if this was true or not, but the phrase was used often on TV medical dramas.

"I think we should check on him."

"We need to make it quick. You check on him while I snag the map."

The narrow road was completely clear of vehicles. Eric shifted gears to come to a stop and let the vehicle idle. He climbed off and headed to the trailer for his map. Stacey followed behind him, her hand lightly touching his arm as they walked.

Sean stirred a little and blinked his eyes.

"We there?"

Eric shook his head. "No. Not yet."

"Where are we going again?" Sean sat up slowly. He looked pale and maybe a little dehydrated.

"A construction site they are making into a fort." Eric opened up the map and began to look over the route he had highlighted in yellow maker days before.

"Did you tell me that?"

"No, he didn't." Stacey forced her brother to recline as she leaned over him.

"Okay, 'cause I was feeling a little hazy there," Sean confessed.

Stacey touched his brow, frowning. "I think you need some water."

"Painkillers would be good. Got anything in that first aid kit?"

As Stacey pulled out the tin box again and began rummaging through it, Eric slid the sleeping Pepe out of his jacket. After being set on the ground, the little dog looked up at him groggily.

"Do your business," Eric ordered before returning his gaze to the map.

Pepe, obviously feeling cranky about being awakened, lifted his leg and tinkled right where he stood.

"Cute dog," Stacey said, actually smiling. "What's his name?"

"Pepe." Eric looked down at the dog. The little guy flopped down on the ground and yawned. "I'm Eric. I don't think I said that before."

"If you did, I forgot," Stacey answered truthfully.

"Wish we could have met under better circumstances." Eric rummaged under the tarp, pulled out a warm bottle of water and handed it to Sean. "I usually try to treat company much better than this."

Sean laughed, the sound thick and a little pained. "Yeah, well, your hospitality sucks. Seriously, who invites zombies to a dinner party?"

"Ha. Ha. Very funny." Gently, Stacey stroked her brother's hair. "Take the aspirin. Drink all the water."

"She's so bossy. Did you notice?" Sean gulped the warm water. "Yuck. It's warm. Where's the ice?"

Ignoring him, Stacey turned her attention to Eric. "I need some water, too. I'm parched."

"Oh, sure. We probably all do." Eric quickly got out two more bottles and poured some into a cap for Pepe after handing one to Stacey.

Stacey gulped down her water and poured the last bit over her reddened face. Her blond bangs hung down limply and her ponytail looked scraggly.

Eric took long pulls off his own water bottle, then leaned back over the map.

"How far?" Stacey gestured to the map.

"Well, if it was a straight shot, we'd be there fairly soon, but there are some towns that I think we should avoid. I have mapped out a very roundabout way to avoid more populated areas. I think we'll get there close to sunset."

"It's about five now. We need to get to shelter before dark."

"How do you know it's five?" Eric noticed she didn't even look at her watch.

"Position of the sun."

"Coop taught us that!" Sean giggled.

Stacey laid her hand on his face again. "I think he's delirious."

"He lost a lot of blood." Eric felt helpless and stared at the other young man sorrowfully.

Biting her bottom lip, she nodded. "Yeah. I know."

Pepe yawned loudly again and leaned against Eric's leg.

Stacey began to rummage around under the tarp, pushing the securing ropes aside and trying not to bother her brother too much. She pulled out the shotgun and checked to see if it was loaded.

"Mind if I hold onto this?"

"Can you handle it?"

"Coop always took us hunting. She's the best shot," Sean said in a drowsy voice. He tossed the empty water bottle into the grass beside the road.

"Hey, no littering," Stacey chided him and went to retrieve the bottle.

"Like the big bad cops are gonna get me," Sean mumbled.

Eric ignored him. "If you can handle the shotgun, take it. I got the revolver and Pepe."

"Yeah. He's a tough little guy. Zombies wouldn't be smart to mess with him," Stacey said giving Pepe an approving look. She wandered into the grass to find the bottle and Pepe followed her looking quite pleased with her commentary on his prowess.

Eric finished studying the map and tucked it away. He felt he had his bearings now. He fished his small pair of binoculars out of his lightweight jacket. Lifting them, he scanned the area. Nothing stirred in the trees or the tall grass. Birds sang and the insects hummed around them, but he didn't see any zombies.

"It looks like we'll be fine on this road until we turn off," Eric decided.

Stacey returned with the bottle in one hand and Pepe in her arms. The shotgun was slung over her shoulder and she looked tired.

Now that the adrenaline rush was over, Eric was feeling exhausted, too. Regardless of his weariness, he knew he had to stay focused on things other than his aching legs from the mad dash earlier and his bleary eyes. Grabbing up one of the extra containers of gas, he turned off the ATV and topped off the tank.

"We don't need to run out of gas at the wrong time," Eric explained.

Stacey snuggled Pepe as she nodded. He licked her cheek and chin happily. Eric was surprised at how easily the dog and the young woman were getting along. Brandy had rarely picked up Pepe.

Once he was done fueling up the ATV, he twisted the cap firmly onto the container and loaded it onto the trailer. Sean moaned low in his sleep and the sound sent a trickle of fear up Eric's spine. It reminded him of the horrible sounds the zombies made. Stacey's twin looked comfortable enough, but his color was off.

"Let's go. Please," Stacey urged. "Pepe's ears are up."

Eric looked toward his dog to see that the little guy was looking around anxiously and sniffing the air. He immediately climbed back onto the ATV and tucked Pepe into his jacket. Stacey slid behind him and grabbed hold of his waist firmly with one arm.

The four-wheel drive vehicle surged forward and hummed over the paved road dragging the trailer behind it. Just as they swept around a curve, Eric saw an old woman standing in the middle of the road in a housedress covered with bright red designs that Eric suspected was actually blood.

"This doesn't look good!" Eric shouted over the wind.

"Don't slow down. Just go around," Stacey urged him. "We can't risk it!"

Eric made sure to give wide berth to the elderly woman. As the ATV swept past her, she reached out to them in silence. She was too far away to snag them and Pepe barked as they passed.

Eric felt Stacey twist around to look back at the woman and he peeked quickly at his mirrors. The gray haired old lady just stared after the vehicle with her gnarled hands held out toward them. "Eric, I think she's alive."

"Shit. I think you're right!"

The old woman would be charging them if she was undead and the big red splotches on her dress now looked more like a deliberate design than blood.

"Eric, we have to get her!"

"Okay, we'll head back for her."

Pepe burst into rapid fire barking. Eric hesitated as he began to pull the ATV about.

Wretchedly, the old woman dropped her arms and turned toward the tree line. Four zombies rushed out of the foliage. She didn't even cry out as they tackled her to the ground.

Eric pulled so hard on the accelerator that they both jerked backward as the vehicle took off.

Stacey screamed. "Oh, God. She was alive! She was alive! We killed her!"

Eric grabbed Stacey's hand firmly and squeezed it. "Listen to me! Listen to me! We didn't know!"

Stacey buried her face in his shoulder, sobbing. "Why won't it stop? Why won't it stop, Eric?"

Caressing her fingers, Eric was at a loss for words. Dread filled him. He was sickened by the truth of their reality. Their chances of survival were slim. "I don't know, but we have to keep going. We have to keep trying to get to a safe place."

Stacey laid her head against his shoulder and he felt her nodding. "I know."

Lapsing into silence, they didn't speak for some time. At one point, Eric was sure she had fallen asleep. She felt heavy against him, but instead of it bothering him, it was a comfort. Eric admired her strength, but the fact that she trusted him so completely touched him.

The sun continued its steady downward path toward the horizon as they traveled. It began to grow cooler and Eric worried about Stacey since she was in shorts and a tank top. He glanced into his rearview mirror to check on her.

Instead of viewing Stacey, he saw Sean rise to his knees. Sean's back was to him and Eric felt his hair rise on his neck. Something wasn't right.

"Stacey, wake up!" Eric grabbed hold of her hand squeezing it. "Stacey!"

Pepe woke up and immediately began to bark. Stacey's head jerked up and she gripped Eric's waist with her hands.

"They're here?"

"No," Eric shouted, tightening his grip on the handlebars. "It's Sean! Something's wrong!"

"What do you mean?"

Stacey swiveled around, one arm still hooked around Eric, as her brother fumbled about on the trailer. When his face came into view, Stacey began to scream. Sean's eyes were milky in death and his mouth contorted grotesquely as he let out a bloodcurdling screech.

18.
Nowhere is Safe

Eric's first impulse was to slam on the brakes, but an image of the now zombified Sean flying off the trailer and crashing into them quickly changed his mind. Instead, he accelerated and saw Sean lose his balance and fall backward onto the blue tarp.

"Oh, God! Oh, God! No! No! No!" Stacey's agonized voice was torn away by the wind, but Eric could feel the trembling of her body against his.

"You're going to have to shoot him, Stacey," Eric yelled at her.

"I can't! It's my brother!"

Pepe twisted around inside Eric's jacket, barking loudly. His little claws scrabbled against Eric's chest as he tried to get leverage.

Meanwhile, the zombie that had been Stacey's twin brother managed to regain its balance and heave itself up onto its knees. Its hands gripped the ropes holding down the tarp as it crawled along the trailer bed toward the two humans on the ATV.

"Stacey, shoot it!"

Eric accelerated again, hoping the wind shear would knock the zombie over and hopefully off the trailer. It didn't work. The creature had its fingers hooked firmly around the ropes and was moving closer.

"Sean, please stop it! This isn't funny! Stop joking!"

"He's not joking, Stacey! Look at his eyes!"

She let out another agonized wail of despair and Eric didn't blame her. He remembered his own horror at seeing Brandy stumbling toward him. It had been almost too much to comprehend or accept.

"Stacey, shoot him! Shoot him or he's going to jump onto us and then we're going to die!"

Pepe kept barking and growling below his chin. Eric felt his stomach knot even more as Stacey remained unmoving behind him.

"I can't use the shotgun," she finally said.

Eric grabbed her hand that was around his waist and guided it to the revolver tucked into his belt. Her fingers were shaking and he squeezed them for a second, then let go. He didn't dare take his eyes off the road.

The sun was moving behind the hills now and the world was darker and colder. The headlights of the ATV illuminated the darkening road before them as the world entered the twilight world of dusk. Stacey pulled the revolver free and tightened her grip on Eric's waist with her other arm as she turned to fire.

The zombie reached the end of the trailer and pulled itself up to its knees. Now it would be easy for it to launch itself over the trailer hitch and onto the back of the ATV. Eric tried not to keep checking the mirrors. It was too easy to imagine the creature jumping onto Stacey.

"Shoot him, Stacey!"

He could feel her body heaving with her sobs, her grip around his waist a painful vise. Daring to check the mirror, he saw the creature rising up, preparing to leap onto Stacey. It opened its mouth and screeched an ungodly sound that ripped at Eric's ears even over the sound of the ATV's engine.

Just as the creature launched itself over the hitch, the gun flashed and the creature jerked backward as the bullet punched through its shoulder.

"In the head!"

"I missed!"

Eric tried to keep his hands steady, guiding the vehicle up the road as it climbed and wound around the hill.

"Shoot him, Stacey! Do it!"

The creature that had been Sean struggled onto its knees and Stacey fired again. The zombie jerked as the bullet grazed its arm, but was not deterred. It leaped across the trailer hitch howling as it made a grab for Stacey.

Eric jerked the ATV to one side in an attempt to avoid the zombie. Stacey clung desperately to Eric as she tried to avoid the creature's clawed hand and not fall onto the asphalt rushing under the wheels of the four-wheel drive. Pepe yelped as the ATV swerved.

The zombie's hand managed to only grip Stacey's shirt for a second then it fell and tumbled onto the road.

"I'm okay! I'm okay!" Stacey's voice was strained.

Eric forced himself to slow down as the ATV continued traveling along the winding road and tried to breathe normally. Pepe, seeming to understand how close they had come to disaster, hunkered down in Eric's jacket and shivered.

Night was coming fast and as they roared around a curve in the road a town in the distance came into view.

It was Ashley Oaks.

"That's it!" Eric said excitedly and brought the ATV to a stop. "I need to double-check the map now."

Stacey climbed off the vehicle, the revolver still in her hand. Shaking, she touched his arm. "Check my back. Tell me he didn't infect me."

Eric felt his gut churn at the thought of losing her. He barely knew her, but she already felt like a friend.

As Stacey twisted around, Eric saw blood on the back of her shirt. With dread in his heart, he reached out nervously. Pulling her shirt up, her long, lean, and muscled back came into view along with the thick band of her sports bra. Her skin was unmarred.

Eric exhaled with relief. "It's okay. You're okay. He didn't even scratch you."

Stacey whirled around, threw her arms around Eric and he felt her tears on his neck.

Gently, he held her close. "You're okay, Stacey."

Pepe squirmed as he was squished between the two of them.

Trying to regain her composure, Stacey took a step back. "I thought for a moment...when my shirt was wet..."

"It's his blood. Not yours."

"I was so afraid." She wiped her tears away as she watched the brilliant pinks and purples decorating the horizon as the night unfurled across the wide Texas sky.

Eric reached out and smoothed her bangs back from her damp forehead. "Stacey, I'm sorry."

Her lips trembled and her nose ran as she nodded mutely. Tears streamed down her dirty, reddened face and she wiped her nose on the back of the hand still holding the revolver.

"I just want to be safe. I just want it to end," she whispered.

"I know. I do, too." Eric sighed wearily. "I thought I was safe until today."

"I'm sorry. We ruined it for you."

"No. No. I was never really safe in the farmhouse. Not really. I always knew that those things could get out of the community center. I was just too scared to take a risk and go somewhere else. I got too comfortable." He laughed bitterly. "So much for comfort now, huh?"

She wiped her nose again and said in a quivering voice, "But you had an escape plan. You saved us."

Eric blushed. He hadn't expected to be a hero. He had just wanted to be ready. "Well, we're not completely safe yet."

In the town below there was light in one central position. Eric checked the map then lifted the binoculars. It took him a moment to figure out exactly where the lights were coming from, but suddenly a construction site in the middle of town swam into view. The site was next to a ten-story red brick building and a smaller building and the entire area was enclosed by a cement wall. Construction trucks that appeared to have sandbags or cement bags shoved under them and between the cabs formed a perimeter just beyond the cement wall. In the gloom before the trucks, the shadows writhed.

"Shit," Eric whispered.

"What is it?"

Eric handed her the binoculars. "Train it on the lights down there."

Stacey lifted the small binoculars with one hand and studied the construction site. "Oh, my God. That's like...what...a hundred zombies? Two hundred?"

Eric took back the binoculars and checked again. He could see how they had used large storage containers to block off the two side streets and corral the zombies directly in front of the fort. The approach along the side streets was probably safest, but he couldn't be sure. The undead throng was massive.

"We're going there?"

"Yeah," Eric answered. "That was the plan."

Suddenly, Pepe howled loudly and startled Eric by popping his head out of his jacket collar. Stacey whirled about and stared down the road. The expression on her face said it all. Eric twisted around in the seat to see Sean running up the road. The zombie's head was lolling to one side and one arm was obviously broken in multiple places, but he was undeterred by his wounds and racing toward them.

Stacey raised the gun and fired once.

The bullet sliced through Sean's forehead and blew out the back of his head. His body fell forward, carried by his momentum and slid to a stop.

Sniffling, Stacey turned to Eric and said, "Please, let's just find someplace safe. Please."

Eric reached out and she handed him the gun. Sliding onto the ATV behind him, she laid her head against his shoulder and wept.

19.
Refuge

The ATV idled at the outskirts of the town of Ashley Oaks. Now that night was coming, it was clear that going into the town was probably not the best idea. Darkness would take away their ability to see any dangers in their surroundings. Going into a house or a building for shelter was also risky. They were at a loss as to what to do.

Stacey shivered from the coolness of the spring night, rubbing her arms to get warm. Eric slid his light jacket off and handed it to her. She pulled it on and stuffed Pepe inside. The little dog buried his face in the crook of her neck and yawned. Eric didn't blame him. He was exhausted, too.

Eric pushed his glasses up on his nose. Sitting in the middle of the road was certainly not a good idea. Any second a zombie may wander into view and they would be forced back into the hills. They had to find somewhere safe to hole up. Lifting his eyes, he saw the perfect refuge.

"The water tower."

"What?"

Eric turned to Stacey. "The water tower. It's like a block away. We can climb the ladder and hang out there tonight."

"That's like one hundred and fifty feet up!"

"Exactly." In the dark, Eric thought the peaked roof of the old water tower looked strangely homey. He was positive this was the perfect place to spend the night.

Stacey warily studied the quaint old water tower. "Can the zombies climb it?"

"I don't think so. They don't seem all that smart the longer they're dead. Remember them pitching head first out of the window?"

Stacey rubbed the top of Pepe's head with her chin thoughtfully. "Okay. I'm cold and I just want to be safe."

"We'll use the tarp to rig a tent or something. I got bedding on the back of the trailer. We'll take supplies up there with us and hang out there tonight or until we can figure out how to get into the fort."

Stacey nodded. "Okay."

Eric shifted gears as Stacey took the revolver from his belt.

"I'll keep a watch out for zombies," she said.

The water tower was not far up a side road that was unpopulated by buildings. The darkness hovering between the trees was intimidating, but Pepe remained quiet and Eric took it as a good sign. The moon was full and the light helped Eric maneuver over the uneven ground.

A large sign that read "Any unauthorized climbing of the tower is a violation of trespassing laws. You WILL be arrested" was set in plain view.

"Guess they had a problem with the kids," Stacey decided.

"Probably the place to hang out in a town like this."

"Yeah, in my town it was the school stadium bleachers. Or under them, I should say," Stacey answered, the added quickly, "Not that I was ever under there!"

Eric laughed as he parked under the tower. "Of course not."

Stacey forced a little smile while sliding off the ATV. Holding Pepe, she stared up at the water tower. Eric turned off the ATV and hopped off. Walking over to the ladder he made note of the chain wrapped around the ladder several times over the rungs about five feet up. Another sign hung from the chain. It had the same threat as the big sign.

"Okay. Let's get this done."

Eric moved quickly to the trailer, ignoring the bloodstains on the blue tarp. Quickly untying the bungee cords and rope, he slid the tarp off. A combination of his luggage and a few pieces he had discovered in the B&B's lost and found were carefully arranged on the trailer filled with supplies. Bright green grocery totes were filled with food staples and water.

"Should we take it all up?"

Eric considered her question, then shrugged. "I don't know."

Stacey studied the tower again. "Not that I want to carry things up there."

Eric took off his glasses and rubbed the bridge of his nose. "Well, we're in the town where we want to be. We just need to figure out how to get into the fort. That could take a few days. Peggy says they are going to clear out the zombies soon."

"But if we take it all up with us and we have to leave fast..."

Eric sighed. "Just half then?"

Stacey bit her bottom lip, then nodded.

Eric began slinging some of the bags onto his shoulders and groaned at their weight. "This is not going to be easy."

"We can use the rope to pull them up."

Embarrassed, Eric blushed. "Oh, yeah."

He grabbed the huge coil of rope he had packed along with the rope and bungees he had used to hold down the tarp.

Stacey grinned at him. "Mr. So Well Prepared doesn't know how well prepared he was."

"Shush, you," he said playfully. "I may be an engineer, but sometimes the simple things confuse me. You know, if it's not something I have to spend hours on and make a dozen designs for."

"Somehow, I believe you."

Eric grinned and headed for the ladder.

The climb to the top was not easy. Getting past the chain had been a little tricky, but not really hard. He was tired and had not eaten since morning so his progress was very slow. His legs and arms burned as he pulled himself up the metal ladder. The cool night air was a welcome relief as sweat poured off his brow. Below, Stacey kept watch with the revolver in one hand and Pepe's leash in the other.

Finally, he reached the top and, gripping the handrails firmly, pulled himself up over the edge and slumped onto the catwalk. The night sky filled his vision and he felt awed by the sight. He was relieved he wasn't afraid of heights as the wind buffeted him and he looked down. The lights from the ATV illuminated Stacey's fit form and Pepe was barely visible.

The catwalk was around three feet wide and quite sturdy. The water tower was from the turn of the last century and very old fashioned. It had a peaked roof and the edges of it partially stuck out over his head giving slight shelter.

Shivering from the cold air, he tied the rope around the sturdy wood railing and dropped it down to Stacey. Thankfully, with the second rope tied to it, it was long enough to reach the ground. Immediately, she began tying bags onto it and Eric hoisted them up.

It took longer than they expected, but Pepe remained calm the entire time. Evidently all the dead were at the construction site. Finally, Stacey killed the lights on the ATV, shoved Pepe into the jacket, and made the long climb to the top. When she reached the catwalk, Eric reached out and helped steady her. She looked tired and overwhelmed in the moonlight.

"Welcome home."

She rolled her eyes, but thankfully slid down to sit on the walkway. Pepe peeked out with fear in his eyes.

"It's okay, Pepe. Just don't get near the edge," Eric said, stroking the little dog's head.

Stacey gently lifted Pepe out of the jacket and set him on the catwalk. Pepe nosed around and dared a brief look over the edge, then darted back to the wall.

Though he was exhausted, Eric knew they needed shelter from the wind. He had been a very thorough packer and pulled out duct tape and wet wipes. Leaving Stacey to recover from the climb, he wiped down the blue tarp she had folded and sent up earlier. He hated to litter, but he dropped the wipes over the edge so she wouldn't have to see the blood. He commenced to use duct tape, the tarp, and some of the rope to construct a makeshift tent. It formed a long narrow shelter for them to sleep in.

Stacey pulled the wet wipes over to her and pulled one out to clean her face and neck.

"Brandy never went anywhere without packing those," Eric commented, a slight hitch in his voice. He began to wrap the rope around the railing posts as he wove a safety net by threading the rope back and forth between the posts.

"What was she like?" Stacey asked after a few minutes.

"Beautiful," Eric answered. He tested the rope to see if it was secure. It held and he was comforted that neither of them would roll off in the middle of the night.

"What else?" Stacey pulled another wipe out and began to clean her arms.

Eric sat back in the shelter and thought for a second. The first word that had come to his mind was *demanding*, but he was loath to say that. He fumbled for something to say that sounded positive, and was surprised to come up empty.

Stacey studied him curiously. "I guess I shouldn't have asked. Sorry."

"It's not that," Eric admitted. "I just...she was very high maintenance. My friends called her a bitch and worse. But I loved her. She was so beautiful and stylish and..." He faltered again. "That sounds so shallow."

Pepe scooted along the side of the water tank and into the shelter. Out of the wind and away from the terrifying view, he relaxed.

Stacey crawled over to the edge of the shelter and he saw her lips were trembling from the cold. "Sometimes we love the wrong people for all the wrong reasons."

Eric felt his throat constrict as he realized her words were true. "I did love her. And, yeah, it was for all the wrong reasons. But..."

Stacey gave him a little hug and crawled over him to sit out of the wind. "I know. I had one of those boyfriends."

Eric sighed. "Sucks, doesn't it?"

"Oh, yeah."

Lapsing into silence, Eric searched through the bags. He handed her some cans of food and a can opener while he searched for the bedding and something for her to wear.

In an hour they were settled in. The comforters from the bed and breakfast were folded over and laid end to end to make a bed for each of them. The king-sized pillow would have to be shared and it was set in the middle of the two beds. Stacey stacked some of the bags and luggage up at her end of the shelter to keep the wind out and Eric kept the other end open just a bit.

"I didn't think cold Beanie Weenies could taste so good," Stacey said after relishing the first bite. She sat with her back against the water tank clad in one of his T-shirts and his pajama bottoms. Pepe was curled up on her lap and she gently stroked his fur.

"Yeah. I think it's the best thing I've eaten in forever," Eric agreed.

He lifted the water bottle he was clutching and sipped the warm water. The moonlight illuminated the world and he could clearly see the outline of the trees and the edges of the town. They were so close now.

"It doesn't seem real," Stacey decided. "Any of this."

"I know."

"If anyone told me a week ago that I would be trapped in the community center with zombies for days, then have to run for my life, shoot my undead brother, ride a quad bike with a guy and his dog, and sack out at the top of a water tower, I would have told them they were freaking nuts."

"I had to kill Brandy," Eric said after a beat.

Stacey regarded him in surprise. "Really?"

"Yeah."

"I'm sorry."

Eric let out a long sigh. "At least she's at peace now."

"I have to think that way about Sean, don't I?"

"It makes it easier," Eric admitted. "Better they be at peace then wandering around."

Stacey slowly lay down and Pepe curled up behind her back, squeezing between the water tower and her body. He was obviously afraid of the fall.

"I know you're right, but..." she curled up and sighed.

Eric lay down, too. They were head to head. She smelled of baby wipes and it was a strangely comforting smell.

"We'll be okay." He believed it now that they were so close to the fort. "We'll find a way to join the others. We'll be safe."

She reached her hand out over the top of the pillow and his fingers closed around it.

It took some time, but finally, they both fell asleep.

20.
Where It All Goes To Hell

Eric woke up to the sound of gunshots in the distance. Pepe began to bark and Stacey sat up sharply. The steady *pop pop pop* of small arms was interlaced with the crack of rifles being fired. Eric scrambled to his feet and shoved past the bags in the opening of the tent. Reaching down, he fumbled through a bag for his binoculars. Finding them, he moved along the catwalk to try to see if he could get a good view of the construction site.

"They must be clearing out the zombies at the fort," Stacey said as she joined him. Pepe was in her arms and his ears were perked up at the sounds in the distance.

The morning light had washed away all the shadows and the town was clearly laid out before them. The downtown area was full of old red brick buildings; several were close to four stories tall. Most appeared to be abandoned. A tall ten-story red brick building towered over the downtown area and the construction site was huddled up against the base of it. Eric could barely make out one area of the fort. What he saw made his heart leap.

A man and a woman were dangling from what looked like a pulley system over the outer rim defense made up of construction trucks. Under them, on the trucks, was a mass of the undead trying to grab them.

"Are they bait?" Eric lowered the binoculars.

She took them and pointed them in the same direction he had. He could see her mouth tense before she handed the binoculars back. "I don't think so. I think something has gone wrong."

Eric returned to gazing through the binoculars at the fort. He tried to figure out exactly what was happening, but the scene was very chaotic. The gunshots continued and zombies toppled over. "I wonder if the zombies figured out how to get in."

Stacey held Pepe closer, snuggling him protectively. The little dog's ears were twitching as he listened to the sound of the weapons firing in the distance. "Eric, if they are getting in where are we going to go?"

Eric glanced toward Stacey hearing the tremor in her voice and reached out to touch her shoulder gently. With all the grime wiped off her face and her hair hanging around her chin, she looked very young and fragile. "We'll be okay. I promise. Somehow we'll find away." He was surprised that he firmly believed his words.

She nuzzled Pepe. "What's happening now?"

For the next thirty minutes, Eric narrated what he witnessed. It was hard to tell exactly what was occurring with his limited view, but it did appear that the fort was winning. The zombies that had clustered under the dangling people were wiped out. The woman undid her harness and dropped down out of view while the dark skinned man was drawn back and lowered out of sight.

The last gunshot echoed away into silence.

"They're lifting a blond woman over the wall. She looks unconscious. And they're lifting a man over, too," Eric said.

"Do you think they're bitten?"

"No. Peggy told me it's the bite that changes people, so I think they know better than to bring in infected people. Maybe they got hurt some other way." Eric rubbed his brow thoughtfully. "Let's get some breakfast, then I'll check and see what's up. If it's clear, maybe we can get to the fort today."

"Okay. Sounds good." She set Pepe down, her shoulders relaxing now that the fort was secure.

The little dog stayed close to the wall as he trotted back to their tent.

They ate ravioli from a can and sipped at the water bottles while Pepe munched on the kibble Eric had packed for him. Stacey sat in silence through most of the meal and Eric didn't blame her. Even though they had slept well, they were both emotionally and mentally exhausted. He felt the urge to lie back down and sleep. His entire body ached from yesterday and he rubbed his sore shoulder with one hand.

Stacey's body was covered in bruises and he felt terrible for her. Her expression was empty and he wondered she was trying not to think about the loss of her family. He left her to her silence and went back to studying the fort.

The activity was calmer now that the zombie assault on the fort was over. In fact, everyone he could spot through the binoculars was grinning. Feeling relieved, he moved back to Stacey's side. Pepe was lying on her lap getting his ears scratched.

"I think we should try to go to the fort. It seems to have calmed down. This may be our best shot," Eric said.

Peering up at him, Stacey said, "I'm scared."

"I know. But we need to try to make it."

Leaning forward a little, she peered at the ground below. It was empty of zombies.

"I just want to feel safe," she said, tears in her eyes. "I'm tired of running away."

"I can try to go alone and send them back for you," Eric offered.

"No!" She grabbed his wrist tightly, tears springing to her eyes. "Don't leave me alone! I'll go with you."

"Stacey, if it's too much for you-"

"No, Eric. I don't want to be alone," she said firmly. "Please. Just let me get my nerve up."

"Okay, Stacey. We'll go when you're ready."

It took her two hours to get her nerves steadied and he let her have the time. There were no more gunshots and every time he checked on the fort, things looked calm. Stacey changed into a pair of his jeans and one of his undershirts. He was surprised that she managed to make the outfit look almost cute when she rolled up the pant legs and tied the shirt at the waist. Brandy wouldn't have been caught dead looking like that.

"My feet hurt so bad." She pulled on her running shoes and managed to tie them, despite her shaking fingers.

"Yeah, I'm pretty sore, too. I've never worked out like this before."

"Do you work out?"

Eric studied her strong arms and powerful legs, then regarded his own thin, but mushy body. "Um. Nope."

She laughed a little. "Then I bet you're really hurting."

"Yeah, well, you're like an Amazon or something. I'm just a mild-mannered engineer."

She motioned to the tent. "Thank God for that."

"I've done much better work than that."

She seemed to relax just a tad. "I'm sure you have."

After a little discussion, they decided to leave their camp on the water tower as a precaution and just take what was still loaded on the trailer. Pepe was stuffed into Eric's jacket once again.   Eric descended first, the revolver tucked into his belt where he could grab it quickly, and Stacey followed him with the shotgun slung over her shoulder.

Pepe kept quiet throughout the ordeal, occasionally peeking out, and then ducking back out of sight. He was obviously unnerved by the height.

When they reached the ground, they were relieved to see the coast was still clear. Eric started up the ATV and Stacey slid on behind him. Eric noted that they were both much more relaxed now that they were on the ground and no zombies had appeared.

The morning coolness was giving away to the noon heat. The jacket was a little warm, but Pepe seemed comfortable enough. Stacey rode with the shotgun in her hand and Eric felt reassured by her determined expression. She was strong despite all they had endured.

They were just two blocks from the water tower when they heard the motorbike.

"Eric!"

"I hear it!" The excitement welling inside of him was intense.

The motorbike came rushing around the corner and Eric swerved to avoid it. The growling bike came to an abrupt stop a few feet from the ATV. There were two men on it and they stared at Eric and Stacey in shock. One of the men, pasty white and hollow eyed, slipped off the motorbike and walked toward them slowly. His companion stayed on the bike and looked uneasily over one shoulder. He was a huge guy with masses of dark hair and golden brown skin.

"Hey," the younger man said to Eric as he approached. "You from that construction site?"

"No, no. We're from out of town. Are you from there?"

The bigger man on the bike shook his head.

"No, man. We're, like, holed up nearby, but we gotta move on. Got company after us," the kid answered and laid a hand on the handlebars.

Eric suddenly felt uneasy. "We're heading to the fort."

"That's cool," the sickly looking man said. "Nice ride."

"Ritchie, you better fucking hurry it up," the bigger man said.

"Shut up, Sergio. I'm dealing with this."

Suddenly, Pepe lifted his head out Eric's jacket and barked angrily.

"Eric," Stacey whispered.

"Ritchie, they're coming!"

"Gimme the quad, bro," Ritchie said to Eric, his eyes growing cold.

"No!" Eric shoved Ritchie's hand off the handlebars.

Ritchie drew his gun quickly and aimed it at Eric's head. "Yeah. Gimme the quad. I need it. We've gotta move on and I need it."

"Eric," Stacey gasped in a terrified voice.

"It's okay," Eric said to her softly. He hoped she would just stay calm and not try anything rash.

Pepe was in a barking fit and it was not directed at Ritchie.

"Dude, they are coming!" Sergio looked back over his shoulder.

"We need the quad to move the others," Ritchie snapped back.

"Just go with us to the fort," Eric pleaded, trying to ignore the gun. "It's safe there."

"No, man. It's full of old people and losers. We're doing our own thing," Ritchie answered tersely.

Eric could see the man's eyes were fully dilated and knew then that he was not dealing with someone with whom he could reason.

"Don't make me shoot you and the girl," Ritchie continued.

Eric was tempted to try to pull his weapon, but he wasn't sure he could shoot anyone still living. Plus, Ritchie could shoot him much faster than he could draw. Reluctantly, he slid off the quad. Stacey slid off with him.

"They're coming!" Sergio whipped out his own gun. "Let's go!"

Ritchie slid onto the ATV and quickly turned it around.

Eric and Stacey both made grabs for the bags on the back of it and both managed to snag two each before the trailer was drawn away. The two thieves then rode off, whooping and laughing.

Pepe hysterically barked.

"We need to run!" Eric broke into a run toward the water tower.

"Not again," Stacey wailed and followed.

They were a block away from the water tower when they heard the howls start behind them. The slap of feet against the pavement spoke of a good number of the dead. Eric dared to look behind him and saw a throng moving rapidly toward them. These zombies had the appearance of the freshly dead.

The bags full of water and food were heavy and Eric considered dropping them. Stacey managed to run ahead of him and rushed down the side road toward the water tower. He was slower than she was and he felt panic rising in him as Pepe's barking became more frenzied.

Eric saw Stacey make it to the ladder and start to climb. Pumping his tired legs as hard as he could, he dared another peek behind him to see that the dead were gaining. Pepe bounced around in his jacket and Eric tried to hoist the bags onto his shoulders as he got closer to the ladder.

"Hurry!" Stacey's voice was frantic.

His heart felt like it was going to burst from exertion, but he forced his body to move faster. Breathless, he managed to reach the bottom of the ladder. It was hard lifting his arms up with the bags on his shoulders and he fought to get up over the chains.

Stacey was above him, the shotgun aimed downward. The bags she had managed to grab were dangling off one of her shoulders and forced her a little off balance.

Struggling, he tried to climb over the chains as Pepe continued to bark furiously.

"Eric!" It was more a shriek than a word.

He had just hoisted himself up onto the rung above the chains when he felt a hand grab his ankle.

"Eric! No!"

Eric grabbed firmly to the rung above him and started to pull himself up. The weight of the creature clinging to his leg made it difficult to climb. Pepe scrambled out of Eric's jacket onto his shoulder, barking fiercely down at the zombie. Everything was happening too fast to process. Eric struggled to even have a rational thought.

Then the worst happened. Pepe fell off his shoulder toward the raging zombie below. His foot slipped off the rung and the bags on his shoulders put so much stress on his grip, he began to slip.

21.
The Beginning of the End

"Pepe!" Stacey and Eric's voices chorused and they both watched in horror as the little dog fell.

With a sharp yelp, Pepe's harness caught at the end of the leash and the small terrier dangled at the end right in front of the zombie. It snarled at the frenziedly barking dog, reached up its other ravaged hand, and batted the dog away like a gnat. Pepe went flying outward with another sharp yelp, swinging high to Eric's left.

As the dog arced away from him on the end of the leash, Eric's heart was beating so hard in his chest that he could feel it thumping against his arm as he managed to get a tighter hold on the rung.

In about that same moment, a bag fell straight past him and slammed into the zombie holding onto his foot. The force of the bag full of cans hitting the zombie knocked its arm free and it staggered away from the ladder. Eric quickly got his foot back onto the rung just as Pepe came swinging back into him and bounced off his ankles.

"Climb!" Stacey's voice was a sharp order.

"You shouldn't have dropped that bag! We need to eat," Eric exclaimed.

"Shut up and climb! It's getting up!"

Eric blinked away the sweat in his eyes, straining to climb higher up on the ladder as Pepe swung back and forth below him dangling from the leash attached to his harness. The added weight of the dog on his wrist, where he always kept the furry boy's leash attached to him, made it hard to lift his arm. The little guy continued to bark hysterically at the zombie struggling to its feet.

The rest of the zombie pack arrived snarling and hissing. Stacey let out a scream that sent shivers down Eric's spine. She quickly scaled down the ladder toward him. He gazed at her in confusion as she hooked one arm around a rung and swiveled about. Lifting the shotgun, Eric realized she was going to fire at something behind him.

"Don't hit Pepe!"

"Hurry up!"

Eric was now a good ten feet off the ground and he kept struggling to climb despite the acute pain in his shoulders from the heavy bags and Pepe dangling from his wrist. The little dog twisted and thrashed in a barking frenzy at the zombies below.

"Eric, hurry! One of them is climbing!"

"Oh, shit!" He heaved himself up a little faster, laboring to move under the items weighing him down. When he reached Stacey's ankles, she reached down, grabbed the leash, and hauled Pepe upwards.

Eric dared a glimpse downward to see the fastest of the zombies struggling to figure out how to climb the rungs. The chains wrapped around the base of the ladder were a determent to its ascension and it was having trouble maneuvering. The rest of the undead assaulted the first zombie, clawing at it as they tried to push past it to the humans above.

Stacey held Pepe tightly against her side and aimed past Eric. He flattened himself against the ladder just as the shotgun barked. The buckshot slammed into the lead zombie and it fell back, one leg strung through a rung and one hand tangled in the chain. The other zombies surged around it, their hands slapping against the ladder, but unable to fathom how to climb.

Stacey, tussling with the last bag on her shoulder and Pepe, stared down in awe at her handiwork.

"Um, move. Before I drop everything or fall," Eric called out.

"Oh." She realized she was stuck and it took a few precious minutes as the zombies jostled each other below for her to finally figure out how to shift everything around so she could climb. Once she was situated, she began to ascend. Eric, his arms now tingling and painful, climbed after her.

A few times he checked beneath him. Each time he was relieved to see the zombies still had no idea how to climb. The dead one tangled up at the bottom of the ladder seemed to confuse them. It was a great relief as he continued to force himself to climb despite his numb fingers and his aching back.

Stacey reached the top and quickly ditched the bag while setting Pepe down. She climbed down to him and reached for one of the bags. He let her hoist it off his shoulder and sighed with relief as she carried it to the platform. She was more physically fit and stronger than he was and he felt a little embarrassed by this fact.

Finally, Eric reached the top. His shoulder was screaming with pain and almost felt dislocated, but he had gotten the precious supplies to the top. He was ridiculously proud of that fact. He flopped over onto the platform and lay there breathing heavily.

Below, the zombies screamed and shrieked in frustration as they pushed each other away from the ladder. Another one had managed to step through the bottom rung and was now entangled with the dead zombie. It kept slamming its fist against the rung above it, but did not comprehend how to climb.

"Thank God they're dumb," Stacey whispered.

Eric watched for a moment, then slowly rolled up to sit with his back against the tank. Pepe crawled onto his lap and shivered against him.

Too exhausted to move, Eric laid his hand over his dog's back.

22.
Trapped

The storm hit two hours later. The dark ominous clouds had been enough warning for them to secure the tent and get their possessions organized. They climbed inside and huddled together with Pepe between them, listening to the wind howl as the rain splattered the tent. Below them, the zombies were unaffected by the rain and continued to moan and struggle with each other.

Both Stacey and Eric were quiet. Eric suspected they were thinking the same thing. How long could they survive up on the water tower? Would the zombies figure out how to climb? Would anyone find them? How long would the food and water last? There were more zombies below than they had bullets for, and they were stuck.

The rain poured off the top of the tent and the wind pulled at the edges, but Eric had done a good job securing it. They remained safe, warm and dry, but their spirits were low.

"The fort is close," Eric said at last. "Peggy said they would send out rescue teams."

Stacey sat next to him, her legs drawn up to her chest, arms folded across her knees. She glanced at him and sighed. "They don't know we're here."

"Yeah, but we can signal them somehow."

"How?" She looked at him pointedly. The tension in her body said it all. She was terrified.

"I brought duct tape. We'll write the world 'help' on the water tower with it. We'll keep a watch for them heading our way and figure out a way to signal them. Fire the gun or something."

"How many shots do we have left in the revolver?"

Eric exhaled. "Three."

"And we have six shells for the shotgun."

Eric rubbed his nose and fiddled with his glasses. "You're right. Can't waste the ammo unless we're positive they're close."

"I think we can make the food last three weeks," she said after a beat.

"Water is going to be harder once it's gone."

"We're on a water tower."

"It's empty I think. For show now." Eric tapped the old-fashioned tank. "But we can rig some water reclamation device for the spring storms. There will be more. Besides, we have to keep positive that they will find us."

Stacey sighed softly and reached out to pet Pepe. "I want to believe you."

"Then do," Eric said firmly. "We'll live through this. I promise."

The next few days they did all they could to secure their little home and make sure the supplies were rationed out. After some exploration, they realized there was no way to access the water tank or make sure it was empty without taking a huge risk to their safety by climbing on top. Reluctantly, they abandoned the idea.

After Eric studied the wind currents and how the surrounding trees broke up the airflow, he picked out a spot on the walkway that would be their lavatory. It was much easier for Eric to relieve himself, but Stacey was terrified at first to position herself between the rails. Eric rigged up a safety harness for her with ropes. He felt bad for her and he made sure to cut all the wet wipes in half to make them last as long as possible. Pepe, meanwhile, had trouble going at first, having been used to going on the grass, but he finally figured out what was expected of him.

The simple things in life suddenly seemed so hard.

Using bottles, some plastic bags and the rest of the tape, Eric managed to come up with a way to trap rainwater. This seemed to reassure Stacey a little. Their food stores concerned them the most and seeing cans of food littering the bottom of the ladder was a reminder of Eric's close brush with death and the sacrifice Stacey had made.

Every day Eric watched the fort through his binoculars. It seemed so close and yet so far away. He watched the people inside the fort clear out the zombie bodies, begin to expand the wall, and go about their daily business. Yet no vehicles came near the water tower. They seemed far away and terribly cut off from the hub of activity and life that was the fort.

It rained often and if there wasn't lightning, Stacey would stand out in the rain. Feeling silly, Eric joined her, but then it was rather nice standing in the warm rain watching the sun pierce through the dark clouds above. One day, he looked over at her to see her face turned rapturously upward. What he had at first considered a plain face with a tiny rosebud mouth, rounded cheeks, turned up nose, and big eyes, suddenly looked quite pretty. Prettier than Brandy had ever looked with her immaculate makeup and fancy tresses. He felt humbled by this revelation. His old world was now long gone and Stacey made the life he had now bearable.

"The rain is great." Stacey grinned at him.

He flushed at her catching him staring at her and nodded slightly. "It feels good. And makes us stink less."

She laughed and he joined her. It felt wonderful.

The rain made it harder for the zombies as the ground became a muddy quagmire. The dead zombie stuck in the bottom rung continued to confuse the other undead and the one that had managed to entangle itself thrashed and moaned.

Eric found himself growing fond of Stacey the more he got to know her. She was actually very nice and sweet. He discovered she liked a lot of the movies and books he did and seemed genuinely interested in his job. Since there was nothing else to do, they would talk for hours while Pepe lay between them getting lavished with attention.

At night, they slept head to head, Pepe taking turns sleeping with each one of them.

The days slipped by.

They grew hungrier and weaker as they carefully rationed out their food and water. Stacey made both of them exercise each day to keep some level of fitness, but they both became more inclined to just sit and watch the clouds float by as they shared their life stories and their former dreams.

The zombies continued to linger at the base of the ladder, trampling the precious cans of food into the ground. Their numbers increased to nearly thirty and the hope of escaping grew dimmer.

Days became weeks.

One night they heard a motorbike nearby and the sound of a girl screaming. The wail, moans and shrieks of a large pack of the dead followed this sound. Eric and Stacey stood and watched the headlight of the motorbike glide up the street then disappear from view as it swerved toward the fort. The dead following caused enough commotion to pull away some of the zombies that had been lingering below.

They heard gunshots in the distance for a short period of time and Eric tried to see what was happening using his binoculars. He was able to discern that something dramatic had occurred, but the fort fought off any danger. Eric remained watching the fort for a long time after Stacey retired. At one point, it looked like a party was happening on top of city hall and he felt a lump in his throat.

So close, but so far away.

The crowd below was down to fifteen zombies after that night, but they were not badly mutilated and were quick on their feet. At times, Stacey and Eric would stare down at the undead and discuss each one individually. They tried to give the zombies a story, even a name, but they eventually stopped when it became too painful to see them as anything other than a zombie. To see the creatures as human only made their own losses more acute.

Food became scarce. Pepe's bag of food was emptied. They began to feed him the meat from the beanie weenies.

The days slipped on. Their rations became smaller.

"We're starving to death," Stacey said one day. "Pepe is, too."

The little dog lay on his side, his ribs showing, looking as weak as they both felt.

"We can't give up," Eric declared.

"No one is coming," she whispered.

"They will."

"But if they don't, we'll die up here."

She stared at him with sunken eyes and his heart broke a little. He hadn't noticed how hollow her cheeks had become. Recognizing he had been in a strange denial despite his terrible hunger pangs and constant thirst, he forced himself to face their true reality.

"What do you want to do?"

"We have enough bullets to..." She covered her face and sobbed.

Pepe whined and scooted closer to her.

"I don't want to die," Eric said to her in a soft, firm voice. Reaching out, he laid his hand on her shoulder.

Stacey drew in a deep breath and gazed at him earnestly. "Either we do it ourselves or we risk running for it. Go down there, shoot them, kill them anyway we can and run for the fort."

Eric studied the remains of their supplies. His small machete was there and the luggage. He could possibly make another weapon out of the metal from the frame of one of the suitcases. Maybe.

"Before we're too starved to move or do anything," Stacey added.

Eric felt tears pricking his eyes as he petted Pepe. The little dog looked fragile and his energy was low. He couldn't bear the thought of his dog starving to death. He couldn't bear the thought of raising his gun and shooting him either.

"Okay," he said finally. "Okay. Let's plan. We'll go tomorrow morning."

Stacey let out an agonized sob and nodded her head.

The rest of the day Eric worked on a makeshift hatchet using the remains of the cans and a metal rod he got out of a rolling suitcase. Stacey practiced swinging the machete as hard as she could and kept double-checking their bags for anything else they could use against the zombies. Pepe watched them with sad eyes, but didn't move much.

That night, they ate an entire can of chicken soup and put the last can aside for breakfast. They fed Pepe the chicken bits out of the soup and savored the broth. Finally, they lay down. Stacey reached out to interlace her fingers with Eric's.

I'm going to kiss her tomorrow, Eric thought and surprised himself with the notion. Yet it seemed natural. They had bonded and she was one of the sweetest, strongest people he had ever met. She was only twenty-two years old but was more stable and confident than the older Brandy had ever been. In the last few weeks he had grown to admire her and consider her a friend. Now, he wanted to give her just one kiss, to show her how much he cared for her. How much she meant to him.

A first and last kiss.

It seemed silly and romantic, yet reassuring.

He wasn't a fool. He knew the reality of the situation. They were going to die tomorrow and he had finally accepted it. But they would go down fighting.

As Eric closed his eyes, he listened to Pepe's breathing and sighed.

Strange, he thought. *I finally found some sort of happiness in this world. And now it's over.*

23.
How It Ends

Eric woke up that last day on the water tower from a hazy dream. In it Brandy was talking to him on the phone and was angry at him for hanging out with Pepe and some girl while she needed a manicure. She kept screaming at him, "Are you there? Can you hear me?"

He blinked at the sunlight streaming in from the opening in the tent and felt confused as he heard a voice call out.

"Hello? Are you there? Can you hear me?"

It was a woman's voice. Gasping, Eric sat up swiftly. Shoving aside the flap of the makeshift tent, he stumbled out onto the walkway and looked over the railing. The zombies screeched and reached up toward him.

A short bus was idling on the street beyond the trees and the thick bushes that lined the area around the water tower. A woman was sitting on top of the roof waving at him.

The morning was crisp and he shivered as the cold sank into his skin.

"Stacey, someone is here!"

He waved at the woman on the bus. "We're here! We're alive!" Then he mumbled, "I hope I'm not dreaming."

Stacey crawled out of the tent clutching Pepe. She blinked her eyes as the bright light hit them and stared at him drowsily. "What?'

"How many are with you?" The woman's voice was loud, but the zombies were still more interested in Eric and Stacey.

Maybe they had to see the person to hone in on them, Eric thought.

The bus was barely visible through the trees and Stacey stared at it incredulously. "Am I dreaming?"

"No, I don't think so. Or we're *both* dreaming!" Eric said with a grin.

Stacey squealed and flung her arm around his waist. "We're saved!"

The woman dressed in jeans, a red sweater, and a hunting jacket stood up and gestured to them. "We're coming to get you! Hang tight. We can't hit them through the tree branches, so we're gonna rush them!"

Eric would never forget the sight that followed. Three men and the woman exited the bus and fearlessly charged into the clearing. The woman, dark hair braided and pinned to the top of her head, came first. She shot a zombie point blank in the face and immediately turned to fire at the next one charging at her.

Meanwhile, a big teddy bear of a man with a round face dressed in what looked kind of like a sheriff's uniform, opened fire with a sawed off shotgun, blasting the nearby zombies clear off their feet.

A young black man wearing a loud red and yellow tracksuit had two revolvers in his hands. With one of the toughest looks on his face Eric had ever seen, he systematically fired at the zombies near the bottom of the ladder.

"I do not appreciate your behavior," Tracksuit said in quite precise tones and shot the head off one of the female zombies.

The last guy, a wizened old guy in a hunting jacket, stood at the edge of the clearing and fired at the zombies rushing at him.

"Jenni," the track suit guy called out. "Behind you!"

The woman jerked around as a zombie rushed out of the trees. She was in the middle of reloading. "Shit!" She dropped to her knees just as the zombie slammed into her and it flipped over her into the mud. Jumping up, she pulled out a machete and slammed it down into its head splitting it open.

"Felix, to your left!" the bigger guy shouted.

Felix, which it turns out was Tracksuit's given name, turned smoothly and nailed a child zombie moving toward him. "Got it, Bill!"

Eric watched in amazement as Jenni rushed after the zombie stuck in the ladder and began hacking away at it with her machete. Bill, Felix, and the unnamed man continued to fire. The area was more infested than Eric had imagined as zombies continued to come out of the trees.

Jenni finished hacking the zombie to pieces and looked up at Stacey and Eric. "Climb down now! Hurry!"

Immediately, Eric and Stacey obeyed her, not bothering to grab anything other than Pepe, the revolver, and the shotgun.

"Ed, cover the east side," Jenni ordered the grizzled old guy before running back to grab her gun. She quickly reloaded, then fired two shots into the head of a legless zombie crawling toward her.

The wizened old hunter nodded and reloaded smoothly before continuing to fire.

Felix and Bill covered the north and west side as Jenni watched the south. The group had obviously worked together before and moved seamlessly as a team.

Eric couldn't climb down fast enough and he felt Pepe trembling against his chest with excitement. The little dog even managed to get out a few weak barks. The gunshots continued below as Jenni motioned for them to hurry. Jenni shoved and kicked at the dead zombie and chopped away at its hand until it dropped off the ladder.

"Gawddamn, fucking, no good, stupid shit eating..." she swore as she kicked it away.

"Jenni doesn't like zombies, Bill. Did you know that?" Felix grinned and reloaded one of his guns quickly.

"You know, I have heard that," Bill answered. "Rumor is she may even hate them."

"Fuck you both," Jenni said with a grin.

There were fewer zombies rushing into the clearing now, but in the distance, they could hear the screech of more coming.

"Hurry up! We haven't cleared this part of town!" Jenni stepped around the ladder and blew the head off a zombie trying to untangle itself from a bush.

Eric finally reached the bottom rungs and leaped down the last few feet. Stacey dropped down beside of him and clutched his hand.

Their four rescuers surrounded them quickly. It was easier to pick off the zombies now that they had some distance between them and the undead. Eric held Stacey's hand and cuddled Pepe close.

"Move toward the bus. Keep close. Don't panic," Jenni ordered.

"Never fear! Super Jenni is here," Felix assured Eric.

"Felix, I'm gonna kick your ass for being a smart ass," Jenni declared.

"Bring it!" Felix flashed a wide smile.

"My money's on Jenni," Bill decided as he fired again.

Ed scowled. "Let's get focused and get out of here, kids."

"Gonna get my ass kicked Jennikillingzombiekungfu-style," Felix singsonged playfully.

"I am so not going to give in to your sick fantasy," Jenni assured him, but she was smirking.

"I'm gonna tell Juan," Bill teased.

"He knows she's his loca. None of us has a chance with the zombie killing machine anymore," Felix decided with a dramatic sigh.

"Like you ever did," Jenni laughed. "Besides, I just rescued your ass last week."

"Enough joking!" Ed looked tense. "Get in the damn bus!"

Eric actually liked the joking. It showed him that the group was confident and sure of what they were doing. The guns continued to fire: zombies of all sizes and shapes fell. The rescuers reached the bus and the doors opened. Eric pushed Stacey in first, then followed her.

The driver was a woman with lots of bushy red hair and there were only two other passengers on board. One was a surly looking black girl, possibly in her late twenties, and the other was a very handsome, but slightly effeminate young man.

"Took you bitches long enough," the young man decided.

"Ken, behave," the girl beside him drawled.

"I'm just kidding, Lenore. Sheesh. Welcome on board the Zombie Rescuemobile. I'm Ken and this is my bestest girl, Lenore."

The girl rolled her eyes.

"Eric and Stacey," Eric said as he slid into a seat next to Stacey.

"We just got rescued, too. Though, not as dramatically as you guys. It was like a movie out there." Ken was obviously impressed.

The doors shut behind their rescuers and they scrambled to take their places. Eric jumped as several zombies reached the bus and banged on the side. There was no way that he and Stacey would have survived if they had attempted to leave this morning. He felt immense relief that they had been rescued and he squeezed Stacey's hand tighter.

"Katarina, let's roll," Ed ordered the driver.

"You got it," she answered, and shifted gears.

Jenni slid into the seat in front of Eric and Stacey and smiled at them. "Glad we found you guys. It was a fluke. Katarina took a wrong turn and we saw the big 'help' on the tower."

Eric sighed with relief and reached out to touch Jenni's arm. "You have no idea how grateful we are."

A shadow passed over Jenni's expression for a second, then she took Eric's hand and squeezed it. "I was rescued once. I do know. I'm glad we found you." She quickly slid out of the seat again and returned to the front of the bus as it rumbled on down the road, leaving the zombies and the water tower behind.

Stacey laid her head on Eric's shoulder and sighed softly. Pepe yawned dramatically and snuggled deeper into his jacket. Feeling relief like he had never experienced before, Eric relaxed and enjoyed the drive to the fort.

They were safe at last.

The fort was nothing like Eric had imagined, but it was still wonderful. The makeshift lock system that let the vehicles entering and leaving the fort move through a series of paddocks was clever and Eric admired the design while taking note of how it could be improved.

When the bus reached the interior of the fort, Jenni quickly disembarked and leaped into the arms of a tall Hispanic man that was waiting for her. She was carried off in his arms, both of them talking in Spanish, and Eric couldn't help but smile at their affection.

Bill and Felix escorted them along with Lenore and Ken to the Ashley Oaks city hall where they were given a lunch of vegetable soup, fresh cornbread, and jello. Nothing had ever tasted so good to Eric. He was relieved to see Pepe eating some soft dog food and slurping down water. Stacey was quiet and ate quickly, but he could understand her apprehension.

They would have died this morning if not for their rescue. They had been so close to the edge of death and now they were safe. It was both a shock and a relief to be at the fort and they were both trying to adjust. People kept stopping by to say hello and Eric was touched by the warmth and friendliness of the fort's inhabitants.

The city secretary met up with them and assigned them their new living quarters. She also promised to have them bumped in line for the shower that was in the basement of the janitor's office in city hall. Her brown hair was pulled back from a pretty face that was free of makeup and had a smattering of freckles across the cheeks and nose. A little boy's hand gripped the leg of her jeans as she rambled off a list of instructions.

"Peggy? It's me! Eric!" He stared at the woman in shock, suddenly recognizing her voice. She looked nothing like he had imagined.

"Oh, Lord. I thought you were dead when you never logged back on!" Her no-nonsense attitude disappeared as she gasped with surprise.

They embraced like old friends and Eric felt tears in his eyes.

He was separated from Stacey after Peggy led her away to find clothes and take a shower. Bill took Eric to meet with Travis, the architect behind the fort construction, and Juan, the head of construction. Both of them were excited to hear he was an engineer and shared some of their plans with him. Eric was amazed at how quickly he absorbed what was going on and made a few suggestions that both Travis and Juan were impressed with.

Finally, he was able to take a shower. Nothing had ever felt so wonderful in his life despite the dank surroundings of the janitor's office and the plumbing banging away in the wall. After he was scrubbed clean, he dressed in jeans and a T-shirt that Peggy had put aside for him. He had been told a Wal-Mart truck had joined the fort on the first day and its inventory had helped significantly. His new clothes were new and stiff and he felt awkward in his new Wrangler jeans.

It was a far departure from his old khaki pants and button-down shirts.

It was like moving through a dream when he walked through the construction site. It was neatly organized into living areas and work areas. Travis had shown him the plans to enter the hotel that loomed over the site and he glanced up at it. The construction crew was going to have to break through the back wall to get into the hotel. Fear of the zombies possibly inside had inspired Travis to build a gated entry just in case of trouble. There was already a small team of men and women working on constructing the padlock to the new entrance.

Slipping into his new home, a tent made of blue tarp, Eric found Stacey lying on a cot with Pepe. They were both sound asleep. Wearily, he rested on his cot and watched them. Both were peaceful in their slumber. Relief filled him as he thought about how lucky he was that they were both safe and with him. Soon, he fell asleep.

When he awoke, Stacey and Pepe were gone.

By evening he had met the people behind the names he had heard from Peggy. Katie was a warm, generous person with beautiful blond curls and a wide smile. She had met him in the lunch line and he liked her immediately. Travis joined them at their table and they spent most of the time talking about construction. Katie stuck around and Travis seemed pleased. Eric wondered if everyone in the fort was finding new connections with each other. He couldn't really blame them. This new deadly world forced everyone to move on and embrace what they had left in life. He had found himself doing that very thing for the last few weeks.

Stacey and Pepe occasionally appeared in his peripheral vision, but he kept being distracted by Travis, Mayor Reyes, Juan and Peggy. They pulled him into their planning session that afternoon and he loved the feeling of being back at work and part of the greater picture.

The sun was setting when he finally made it back to the tent. Stacey and Pepe were not there and he felt lonely without them. Sitting on his cot, he took a deep breath and exhaled slowly.

In one short day, his whole world had changed again. He and Stacey were still alive, they were safe in the fort, and Pepe was going to be okay. They had made it just like he had hoped and promised. Now he felt lonely without them and he sat in silence in the blue tent that was bigger, but just as makeshift as the old one on the water tower. He suddenly felt homesick for the water tower.

"You're popular," Stacey said from the entry. She stepped in and let the flap fall back behind her.

Pepe bounced over to Eric and wagged his tail. Already he looked so much better.

He plucked Pepe off the ground to pet him. "They're picking my brain for the construction of the fort defenses."

Stacey gazed at him with an expression that was hard to fathom. Dressed in a yellow summer dress, her short straight hair falling to just above her shoulders, she looked pretty, fresh, and young. Folding her arms over her breasts, she gave a little sigh.

"Is something wrong?"

She shrugged her bony shoulders. "I'm glad to be here, but it feels weird now."

"Weird?" He regarded her curiously, but he thought he understood.

"It was just us out there. You, me, Pepe. We felt like a little family or something. But here..."

Eric set Pepe aside and stood up. "Stacey..."

"Look, I know I'm like six years younger than you. I probably seem very stupid and young compared to Brandy. And I know you were taking care of me because you're a good guy. You don't have to share-"

Eric kissed her.

Startled, she stopped talking, then wrapped her arms around his neck. They clung to each other for a long moment and when they parted, they were both crying.

"Why didn't you do that before?" she asked in a tremulous voice.

"I didn't want you to think I was doing it because we were going to die," Eric admitted.

Stacey laughed, wiping her tears away. "Well, you did promise me we wouldn't die. And you were right."

Eric stroked her hair gently. "I always keep my promises."

"I just thought that now that we're here and-"

"Stacey, I want you here with me and Pepe."

She peered up at him through her tawny eyelashes, slightly smiling. "Promise?"

Eric laughed and kissed her lips again. "I promise."

Pepe whined at their feet. Stacey stooped, picking him up.

"See, Pepe, wants you here, too. We're a little family." Eric wrapped his arms around both of them as Pepe squirmed around trying to lick them both at the same time.

As the sounds of construction continued around them, the chatter of voices wafted on the evening breeze, and the distant sound of thunder rumbled, they looked at each other, smiled, and knew they were finally home.

—*Author photo courtesy of Mary Milton*

Rhiannon Frater is the award-winning author of the *As the World Dies* trilogy *(The First Days, Fighting to Survive, Siege,)* and the author of three other books: the vampire novels *Pretty When She Dies* and *The Tale of the Vampire Bride* and the young-adult zombie novel *The Living Dead Boy and the Zombie Hunters*. Inspired to independently produce her work from the urging of her fans, she published *The First Days* in late 2008 and quickly gathered a cult following. She won the Dead Letter Award back-to-back for both *The First Days* and *Fighting to Survive,* the former of which the Harrisburg Book Examiner called 'one of the best zombie books of the decade.' Tor is reissuing all three *As the World Dies* novels. You may contact her by sending an email to rhiannonfrater@gmail.com or visit her online at rhiannonfrater.com. You can find out more about the *As the World Dies* trilogy and world by visiting astheworlddies.com.

Made in the USA
Lexington, KY
30 December 2012